Thomas Gordon Hake, Alice Christiana Thompson Meynell

The Poems of Thomas Gordon Hake

Thomas Gordon Hake, Alice Christiana Thompson Meynell

The Poems of Thomas Gordon Hake

ISBN/EAN: 9783337408589

Printed in Europe, USA, Canada, Australia, Japan

Cover: Foto ©Andreas Hilbeck / pixelio.de

More available books at **www.hansebooks.com**

THE POEMS OF
THOMAS GORDON HAKE

SELECTED

WITH A PREFATORY NOTE BY

ALICE MEYNELL

AND A PORTRAIT BY

DANTE GABRIEL

ROSSETTI

LONDON: ELKIN MATHEWS AND
JOHN LANE
CHICAGO: STONE AND KIMBALL
1894

PREFATORY NOTE

THE Poems in this collection are chosen from volumes published at intervals over more than fifty years—among them *The Piromides*, issued in 1839, *Madeline*, reviewed by Dante Gabriel Rossetti in the *Academy* in 1871; *Parables and Tales*, to which Rossetti gave a *Fortnightly Review* article in 1873; down to *The New Day*, dated 1890; together with verses which will be new even to the readers of the hitherto published works.

Dr. Hake has a solemn and distinct note, little confusible with the other notes of the concerted song of poets. Only nine years younger than the century, he inherited, by right of his time and place, a tradition of deep composure—poetry aloof from the peril of excitement which knows neither how to contain nor how to express itself. Dr. Hake's expression always implies long intention, deliberate decision. The verse is a consequence long foreseen.

The emotion of moments lacks indeed no swiftness of passage, but we are made aware that it had a past of experience and has a future of power. It was not a gust born of the moment and then no more. Poetic passion must be like a wind; thou canst not tell whence it cometh nor whither it goeth; but surely it appeared with an approach and disappeared with a departure; it was a thing of transitory phase, but not of transitory life. Essentially durable and spiritual is the passion of those infrequent poems in which this poet, raising himself from the attitude of meditation, gathers his word into intenser action.

He has emotion which is thus proved true. For the proof of the authenticity of his thought, also, the reader will look into his own experience as he reads.

Il poeta mi disse : Che pense?

The question which Virgil asked of Dante is a poet's question. The world takes it as generally the reader's question; but it is emphatically the poet's. Now, the thought to which Dr. Hake appeals in his reader's mind is unquestionably not an easy nor an obvious one. In saying this we assign to the reader of poetry some part of the writer's responsibility, some part of his honour. Or, if this is too much to say, the reader is at any rate responsible for choosing his poet. And if a poet is worth reading at all, he is to be trusted both with the importance and with the distinctness of his own thought.

The exceeding solemnity of what we have called Dr. Hake's note—and it is as indescribable and as peculiar as the note of a voice—suggests a further meaning, even an allegory, where in fact he had no intention of proposing anything beyond the text. The more does this illusion occur, perhaps, because Dr. Hake tells a story—a story of events—in most meditative stanzas. He writes movingly of dreams and sleep; and his study of these has added to all or almost all his verse something of the ecstasy of dreams.

ALICE MEYNELL.

February 1894.

CONTENTS

CONTENTS

ALONE

Loved, wedded, and caressed,
Although her children died
She still seemed doubly blest,
Her helpmate at her side
More dear than all the rest!

But sorrow did not kill
The thought of those so dear,
Who all her feelings fill,
As though still with her here
To play about her still.

Her little children's fate
She never could recall,
Yet lived she desolate,
For she had lost them all,—
And then she lost her mate.

A

When came that hour of woe
 And all she loved was gone,
Not sorrow's keenest blow
Left her fond heart alone ;
No parting could it know.

Nigh her he still appears,
The early times so cling ;
Her simple heart still hears
Her children laugh and sing
As in the happy years.

The dead to her remain ;
She heeds each gentle sound
Of theirs within her brain,
And answers smiling round :
' Sweet love, say that again ! '

Is it that angels dwell
In that lone mother's breast ?
She knows not what befell,
And so is doubly blest :
No more her heart can tell.

OLD SOULS

I

THE world, not hushed, lay as in trance;
   It saw the future in its van,
And drew its riches in advance,
   To meet the greedy wants of man;
Till length of days, untimely sped,
Left its account unaudited.

II

The sun, untired, still rose and set,—
   Swerved not an instant from its beat:
It had not lost a moment yet,
   Nor used in vain its light and heat;
But, as in trance, from when it rose
To when it sank, man craved repose.

III

A holy light that shone of yore
    He saw, despised, and left behind :
His heart was rotting to the core
    Locked in the slumbers of the mind
Not beat of drum, nor sound of fife,
Could rouse it to a sense of life.

IV

A cry was heard, intoned and slow,
    Of one who had no wares to vend :
His words were gentle, dull, and low,
    And he called out, ' Old souls to mend ! '
He peddled on from door to door,
And looked not up to rich or poor.

V

His step kept on as if in pace
    With some old timepiece in his head,
Nor ever did its way retrace ;
    Nor right nor left turned he his tread
But uttered still his tinker's cry
To din the ears of passers-by.

VI

So well they knew the olden note
 Few heeded what the tinker spake,
Though here and there an ear it smote
 And seemed a sudden hold to take;
But they had not the time to stay,
And it would do some other day.

VII

Still on his way the tinker wends,
 Though jobs be far between and few;
But here and there a soul he mends
 And makes it look as good as new.
Once set to work, once fairly hired,
His dull old hammer seems inspired.

VIII

Over the task his features glow;
 He knocks away the rusty flakes;
A spark flies off at every blow;
 At every rap new life awakes.
The soul once cleansed of outward sins,
His subtle handicraft begins.

IX

Like iron unannealed and crude,
    The soul is plunged into the blast ;
To temper it, however rude,
    'Tis next in holy water cast ;
Then on the anvil it receives
The nimblest stroke the tinker gives.

X

The tinker's task is at an end :
    Stamped was the cross by that last blow.
Again his cry, 'Old souls to mend !'
    Is heard in accents dull and low.
He pauses not to seek his pay,—
That too will do another day.

XI

One stops and says, 'This soul of mine
    Has been a tidy piece of ware,
But rust and rot in it combine,
    And now corruption lays it bare.
Give it a look : there was a day
When it the morning hymn could say.'

OLD SOULS

XII

The tinker looks into his eye,
  And there detects besetting sin,
The decent old-established lie,
  That creeps through all the chinks within.
Lank are its tendrils, thick its shoots,
And like a worm's nest coil the roots.

XIII

Like flowers that deadly berries bear,
  His seed, if tended from the pod,
Had grown in beauty with the year,
  Like deodara drawn to God;
Now like a dank and curly brake,
It fosters venom for the snake.

XIV

The tinker takes the weed in tow,
  And roots it out with tooth and nail;
His labour patient to bestow,
  Lest like the herd of men he fail.
How best to extirpate the weed,
Has grown with him into a creed.

OLD SOULS

XV

His tack is steady, slow, and sure :
   He plucks it out, despite the howl,
With gentle hand and look demure,
   As cunning maiden draws a fowl.
He knows the job he is about,
And pulls till all the lie is out.

XVI

'Now steadfastly regard the man
   Who wrought your cure of rust and rot !
You saw him ere the work began :
   Is he the same, or is he not ?
You saw the tinker; now behold
The Envoy of a God of old.'

XVII

This said, he on the forehead stamps
   A downward stroke and one across,
Then straight upon his way he tramps;
   His time for profit, not for loss;
His task no sooner at an end
Than out he cries, 'Old souls to mend !'

OLD SOULS

XVIII

As night comes on he enters doors,
  He crosses halls, he goes upstairs,
He reaches first and second floors,
  Still busied on his own affairs.
None stop him or a question ask;
None heed the workman at his task.

XIX

Despite his cry, 'Old souls to mend!'
  Which into dull expression breaks,
Not moved are they, nor ear they lend
  To him who from old habit speaks;
Yet does the deep and one-toned cry
Send thrills along eternity.

XX

He gads where out-door wretches walk,
  Where outcasts under arches creep;
Among them holds his simple talk.
  He lets them hear him in their sleep.
They who his name have still denied,
He lets them see him crucified.

XXI

On royal steps he takes a stand
  To light the beauties to the ball;
He holds a lantern in his hand,
  And lets his simple saying fall.
They deem him but some sorry wit
Serving the Holy Spirit's writ.

XXII

They know not souls can rust and rot,
  And deem him, while he says his say,
The tipsy watchman who forgot
  To call out 'Carriage stops the way!'
They know not what it can portend,
This mocking cry, 'Old souls to mend!'

XXIII

While standing on the palace stone,
  He is in workhouse, brothel, jail;
He is to play and ball-room gone,
  To hear again the beauties rail;
With tender pity to behold
The dead alive in pearls and gold.

XXIV

In meaning deep, in whispers low
   As bubble bursting on the air,
He lets the solemn warning flow
   Through jewelled ears of creatures fair,
Who, while they dance, their paces blend
With his mild words, ' Old souls to mend !'

XXV

And when to church their sins they take,
   And bring them back to lunch again,
And fun of empty sermons make,
   He whispers softly in their train ;
And sits with them if two or more
Think of a promise made of yore.

XXVI

Of those who stay behind to sup,
   And in remembrance eat the bread,
He leads the conscience to the cup,
   His hands across the table spread.
When contrite hearts before him bend,
Glad are his words, ' Old souls to mend

XXVII

The little ones before the font
   He clasps within his arms to bless ;
For Childhood's pure and guileless front
   Laughs back his own sweet gentleness.
' Of such,' he says, ' my kingdom is,
For they betray not with a kiss.'

XXVIII

He goes to hear the vicars preach :
   They do not always know his face,
Him they pretend the way to teach,
   And, as one absent, ask his grace.
Not then his words, ' Old souls to mend !'
Their spirits pierce or bosoms rend.

XXIX

He goes to see the priests revere
   His image as he lay in death :
They do not know that he is there ;
   They do not feel his living breath,
Though to his secret they pretend
With incense sweet, old souls to mend.

XXX

He goes to hear the grand debate
  That makes his own religion law ;
But him the members, as he sate
  Below the gangway, never saw.
They used his name to serve their end,
And others left old souls to mend.

XXXI

Before the church-exchange he stands,
  Where those who buy and sell him, meet :
He sees his livings changing hands,
  And shakes the dust from off his feet.
May be his weary head he bows,
While from his side fresh ichor flows.

XXXII

From mitred peers he turns his face.
  Where priests convoked in session plot,
He would remind them of his grace
  But for his now too humble lot ;
So his dull cry on ears devout
He murmurs sadly from without.

XXXIII

He goes where judge the law defends,
  And takes the life he can't bestow,
And soul of sinner recommends
  To grace above, but not below ;
Reserving for a fresh surprise
Whom it shall meet in Paradise.

XXXIV

He goes to meeting, where the saint
  Exempts himself from deadly ire,
But in a strain admired and quaint
  Consigns all others to the fire,
While of the damned he mocks the howl,
And on the tinker drops his scowl.

XXXV

Go here, go there, they cite his word,
  While he himself is nigh forgot.
He hears them use the name of Lord,
  He present though they know him not.
Though he be there, they vision lack,
And talk of him behind his back.

XXXVI

Such is the Church and such the State.
  Both set him up and put him down,—
Below the houses of debate,
  Above the jewels of the crown.
But when 'Old souls to mend!' he says,
They send him off about his ways.

XXXVII

He is the humble, lowly one,
  In coat of rusty velveteen,
Who to his daily work has gone;
  In sleeves of lawn not ever seen.
No mitre on his forehead sticks:
His crown is thorny, and it pricks.

XXXVIII

On it the dews of mercy shine;
  From heaven at dawn of day they fell;
And it he wears by right divine,
  Like earthly kings, if truth they tell;
And up to heaven the few to send,
He still cries out, 'Old souls to mend!'

VENUS URANIA

Is this thy Paphos,—the devoted place
  Where rests, in its own eventide, thy shrine?
  To thee not lone is solitude divine
Where love-dreams o'er thy waves each other chase
And melt into the passion of thy face!
  The twilight waters, dolphin-stained, are thine;
  The silvery depths and blue, moon-orbed, entwine,
And in bright films thy rosy form embrace,—
Girdling thy loins with heaven-spun drapery
Wove in the looms of thy resplendent sea.
  The columns point their shadows to the plain
  And ancient days are dialed o'er again;
The floods remember: falling at thy feet,
Upon the sands of time they ever beat.

THE CRIPPLE

I

A BROOK beneath the hill-side flows
　　Amid the downs, whose chalky sweep
A scant though tender herbage grows,
　　Cropped close by scattered flocks of sheep.
And there a group of huts is seen
Dotted along a village green.　　　⁚

II

Yet, buildings of a statelier look
　　That poor sequestered valley grace :
An inn beside the village brook ;
　　A church beside the burial-place.
Save at the park, the trees are few ;
Still the old graveyard has its yew.

B

III

Beyond the park, the ring-dove's haunt,
   Red bricks insult the smokeless sky :
There stands the workhouse, bare and gaunt,
   Like the drear soul of poverty,
And frowns upon a mossy fen,
Where willows crouch like agéd men.

IV

All life surrounds the roadside inn,
   The home of welcome and good cheer,
Where barmaid scores the gill of gin
   And oft-repeated pot of beer :
Unlike the fashion of the town—
To drink and fling the money down.

V

The wife, with eggs and milk for sale,
   Wrapt in the coat of her good man,
Stops there and takes her drop of ale
   While waiting for her empty can,
And, nodding at the landlord's sport,
Keeps for the last her smart retort.

VI

The goodman, always on his mare,
  Stops with familiar nod and wink,
And bids the landlord with him share
  His amber draught of foamy drink;
With chuckling joke concludes his say,
And laughs when out of hearing's way.

VII

There with his team the carter stays,
  The water-trough his horses find;
Worn out himself, he little says—
  No fun has he to leave behind.
Dull to the merry toper's call,
His team he follows to their stall.

VIII

The squire, addicted not to chat,
  But seldom draws the rein or speaks;
Seeing the landlord touch his hat,
  Into a quiet trot he breaks;
Though at election, oft he stops
To praise the children and the crops.

IX

Between the horse-trough and the door
  A widow's son was wont to stand.
He was a cripple, crutched and poor,
  Yet always ready with a hand,
Pleased when on trifling errands sent,
With little recompense content.

X

So oft a copper coin the boy
  Would earn, that helped to buy him bread,
Too glad to get a light employ :
  The parish all his mother's dread.
Hard had she worked to earn him food
Through all her weary widowhood.

XI

More did that mother love her son
  Than had he been the fairest born ;
He was her pride to look upon,
  Though shrunk of limb and feature worn :
May be she loved him all the more
For that his legs were crookt and sore.

XII

As a wrecked vessel on the sand,
  The cripple to his mother clung :
Close to the tub he took his stand
  While she the linen washed and wrung ;
And when she hung it out to dry
The cripple still was standing by.

XIII

When she went out to char, he took
  His fife, to play some simple snatch
Before the inn hard by the brook,
  While for the traveller keeping watch,
Against the horse's head to stand,
Or hold its bridle in his hand.

XIV

Sometimes the squire his penny dropped
  Upon the road for him to clutch,
Which, as it rolled, the cripple stopped,
  Striking it nimbly with his crutch.
The groom, with leathern belt and pad,
E'en found a copper for the lad.

XV

The farmer's wife her hand would dip
  Down her deep pocket with a sigh;
Some halfpence in his hand would slip,
  When there was no observer nigh;
Or give him apples for his lunch,
That he loved leisurely to munch.

XVI

But for the farmer, what he made,
  At market table he would spend,
And boys who used not plough or spade
  Had got the parish for their friend;
He paid his poor rates to the day,
So let the boy ask parish-pay.

XVII

Yet would the teamster feel his fob,
  The little cripple's heart to cheer,
Himself of penny pieces rob,
  That he begrudged to spend in beer;
His boy, too, might be sick or sore,
So gave he of his thrifty store.

XVIII

A sheep-worn walk along the brook
  The cripple loved, for there the gush
Of water thralled him as it shook
  The ragged roots of the green rush,
Which with its triple flowers of pink
Stood ripe for gathering at the brink.

XIX

The heather bristles round the knoll,
  Where inlaid moss and leaflets blend :
'Tis there he sits and ends his stroll,
  His crutch beside him as his friend,
And looks upon the other bank,
Where blue forget-me-not grows rank ;

XX

Where purple loosestrife paints the sedge ;—
  Where bryony and yellow bine,
Locked in blush-bramble, climb the hedge,
  And white convolvulus enshrine.
Nestled in leaves, they all appear
Each other's flowers to nurse and rear.

XXI

There mused he like a child of yore—
    By Nature's simple teachings led;
The cog and wheel of human lore
    Not yet were stirring in his head;
The Shaper of his destiny
He felt was smiling from the sky.

XXII

There with soft notes his fife he fills,
    A mere tin plaything from the mart,
But his thin fingers as it thrills,
    To that poor toy a grace impart,
While it obeys his lips' control,
And is a crutch unto his soul.

XXIII

At church he longed his fife to try,
    Where oboe gave its doleful note,
Where fiddle scraped harsh melody,
    Where bass the rustic vitals smote.
Such old-day music was in vogue,
And psalms were sung in village brogue.

XXIV

His cheerful ways gave many cause
  For wonder; such ill-founded joy
To others' mirth would give a pause:
  His soul seemed lent him for a toy,
Though on his infant face was age
To mark him for life's latter stage.

XXV

Dead is his crutch on moping days—
  'Tis so they call his sickly fits,
When by his side his crutch he lays,
  And in the chimney-corner sits,
Hobbling in spirit near the yew
That in the village churchyard grew.

XXVI

Ah! it befell at harvest-time,—
  Such are the ways of Providence,—
That the poor widow in her prime
  Was fever-struck, and hurried hence;
Then did he wish indeed to lie
Between her arms and with her die.

XXVII

Who shall the cripple's woes beguile?
　Who earn the bread his mouth to feed?
Who greet him with a mother's smile?
　Who tend him in his utter need?
Who lead him to the sanded floor?
Who put his crutch behind the door?

XXVIII

Who set him in his wadded chair,
　And after supper say his grace?
Who to invite a loving air
　His fife upon the table place?
Who, as he plays, her eyes shall lift
In wonder at a cripple's gift?

XXIX

Who ask him all the news that chanced—
　Of farmer's wife in coat and hat,
Of squire who to the city pranced—
　To draw him out in lively chat?
This flood of love, now but a surf
Left on a nameless mound of turf.

XXX

Some it made sigh, and some made talk,
   To see the guardian of the poor
Call for the boy to take a walk,
   And lead him to the workhouse door:
With lifted hands and boding look
They watched him cross the village brook.

THE INFANT MEDUSA

By Poseidon

I LOVED Medusa when she was a child,
   Her rich brown tresses heaped in crispy curl
   Where now those locks with reptile passion whirl,
By hate into dishevelled serpents coiled.
I loved Medusa when her eyes were mild,
   Whose glances, narrowed now, perdition hurl,
   As her self-tangled hairs their mass unfurl,
Bristling the way she turns with hissings wild.

Her mouth I kissed when curved with amorous spell,
Now shaped to the unuttered curse of hell,
   Wide open for death's orbs to freeze upon ;
Her eyes I loved ere glazed in icy stare,
Ere mortals, lured into their ruthless glare,
   She shrivelled in her gaze to pulseless stone.

THE LILY OF THE VALLEY

I

THERE was a wood, it does not change,
　　Not while the thrush pipes through its glades,
And she who did its thickets range
　　Has willed her sunbeam to its shades.
There still the lily weaves a net
With bluebell, primrose, violet.

II

The wood is what it was of old,
　　A timber-farm where wildflowers grow.
There woodman's axe is never cold,
　　That lays the oaks and beeches low.
But though the hand of man deface,
The lily ever grows in grace.

III

Of loving natures, proudly shy,
   The stock-doves sojourn in the tree,
With breasts of feathered cloud and sky,
   And notes of soft though tuneless glee:
Hid in the leaves they take a spring,
And crush the stillness with their wing.

IV

The wood is deep-boughed, and its glade
   Has ruts of waggon to and fro;
Yet where the print of wheel is made
   The bracken ventures still to grow;
And where the foot of man may goad,
The ants are toiling with their load.

V

The wood, even old in olden days,
   No longer alters with the year.
The gnarléd boughs, to Nature's ways
   Inured, their honours mildly bear.
And she who there has fixed her beam
Is still remembered as a dream.

VI

There many a legend of the wood
   Has hovered from the olden time,
When, with their sooths and sayings good,
   Men told not of its youth or prime.
The hollow trunks were hollow then,
And honoured like the bones of men.

VII

There like nine brethren, Nature's own,
   Nine trees within a circle stand,
And to a temple's shape have grown,
   Each trunk a column tall and grand.
And, there, a raven-oak uprears
Its dome that whitens with the years.

VIII

'Mid these, while on the earth at play,
   She, the true beam of living spring,
The playmate of the lily's ray,
   Learnt of the piping thrush to sing.
The lily's leaves were then her nest,
Its buds half-nestled in her breast.

IX

To her whose beam was lily-bright
  'Neath brakes that hide the sky above,
A primrose seemed a holy sight :
  Loveless itself, it taught her love.
It was her welcome to the bowers,
And lured her fingers to its flowers.

X

Not yet to her was Nature's age
  In gnarled and hollow shapes revealed :
The buds and leaflets stamped her page,
  And all that Death could say concealed.
To gnarled and hollow Nature cold,
She had not caught the sense of old.

XI

When folk who gossiped thereabout
  Asked the child's name,—the child so pale,—
With looks that gave a sweetness out,
  She answered, ' Lily of the Vale.'
Not then her eyes had dew-drops shed
In early tribute to the dead.

XII

Alas! her parents came to die ;
   She was not then too young to weep.
Through all the wood was heard her cry ;
   Till with her sobs she fell asleep,
And o'er her slumber shot those beams
That with a shiver visit dreams.

XIII

The lilies in their nest had died,
   Violets were closed, their petals crushed,
The bracken-stalks were parched and dried,
   The flowers she loved no longer blushed.
Towards sorrow did her soul ascend ;
Her dawn of joys was at an end.

XIV

The oak spread o'er her troubled sleep,
   She sees a gnarled and hollow form
Whose riven branches seem to creep,—
   Loosed from their long-enchanted storm,
And like a phantom in the air
It sets on her its naked stare.

c

XV

That oak she oft had seen before,
　And in its empty cell had played,
But felt not it was bald and hoar
　With the green ivy o'er it laid.
Now have those thoughtless moments flown
And with the oak she is alone.

XVI

Then she beheld o'ersnowed with age,
　Her grandsire trembling in the wind,
Smiling on her, his heritage,
　The child his son had left behind.
Old was she now, for she could see
Her grandsire agéd like the tree.

XVII

As flowers her eager heart once fired
　With love for things that came and passed,
These visions in her soul inspired
　An awe of sadder things that last:
The sire by age and trouble bent,
The tree by storm and lightning rent.

XVIII

Sleep left her, but her startled gaze
  Met not the sire beside the oak
There standing in its leafless maze
  As in her dream, when she awoke.
Where was the sire? She could not see
The face that smiled beside the tree.

XIX

And then she towards the cottage ran,
  There was the sire in his retreat,
There was he still,—the agéd man,—
  Calm-sitting on his mossy seat,
And of her dream, as true, she spoke
While resting 'neath the raven-oak.

XX

He told her how the raven reared
  Her young ones on the leafy crest,
And now the oak by lightning seared
  Could give no shelter for a nest.
With this her simple thoughts he led
To how the bird the prophet fed.

XXI

Then did she feel that he was poor;
    That on a scanty crust he fared.
She longed to see within his door
    The frugal meal she oft had shared,
And prayed the raven in her need
To do for them the loving deed.

XXII

Through every grove she poured her lay,
    This drooping Lily of the Vale;
As through the brakes she took her way
    She told the thrush her touching tale,
And bade it in her service press
The bird that waits on man's distress.

XXIII

So, like a creature on the wing,
    She spoke her griefs to all she met.
The thrush had taught her how to sing
    Soft notes to all things living set;
Conies that peeped from out the grass,
They had no fear and let her pass.

XXIV

She thought the thrush with mellow song
  Would answer to her simple strain,
She thought the other birds would throng
  To bring the raven back again,
But not to her the raven sped
Who brought from heaven the prophet's bread.

XXV

Meantime her grandsire day by day
  Was hungered, hopeless though he smiled,
For he would hide his pains away
  From her, the watchful, loving child.
She saw him sink upon his bed
Not by the kindly raven fed.

XXVI

Again through brake and bush she flew ;
  Beyond the wood there lay the field
And paths unknown broke on her view ;
  Must she to childish terror yield ?
She looked at heaven and saw its scope,
Taught by her mother there was hope.

XXVII

And then she to her mother said,
  'Can God the prophet's raven spare ?
For grandsire lies upon his bed,
  And cannot earn his daily fare.
All father's work he leaves undone,
And says I soon shall be alone.'

XXVIII

Then she went on and seemed to tread
  The buoyant air that past her blew,
But cast her looks about in dread,
  As o'er the footless path she flew.
At last she stayed to breathe her fear,—
All was so strange, and no one near.

XXIX

And then she to her father said,
  'Can God the prophet's raven spare ?
For grandsire lies upon his bed,
  And cannot earn his daily fare.
He leaves the work you left undone,
And says I soon shall be alone.'

XXX

Her slack'ning pace now plainly told
  The way was long for timid feet.
She felt her heart no longer bold :
  Oft she looked back her wood to greet.
Her wood from sight a moment gone,
She felt herself indeed alone.

XXXI

She stood where hills and valleys blend ;
  One struggle more, and heaven seemed nigh.
Beyond where fields and woods ascend,
  She saw a mansion towering high,
A noble lady's home, that seemed
To her the heaven of which she dreamed.

XXXII

'Could I,' she thought, 'that hill ascend,
  Then should I see the lady's face.
She lives above, where troubles end,
  And I have found her heavenly place.
God gives her plenty for the poor,
Who come home laden from her door.'

XXXIII

She looked till flashed across her dreams
  A sight that all her spirit fired ;
A form behind the window gleams,—
  Could it be she so long desired ?
Through windows in that stately pile,
She thought she saw a human smile.

XXXIV

And then she to the lady said,
  ' Can God the prophet's raven spare ?
For grandsire lies upon his bed,
  And cannot earn his daily fare.
All father's work he leaves undone,
And says 1 soon shall be alone.'

XXXV

The mansion stood against the sun :
  There long she looked for her reply.
The ball of fire whose course had run,
  Filled with its red the western sky,
'Twas awful to her childish sight :
She turned her troubled steps for flight.

XXXVI

Dared she but enter at the gate
  To reach that mansion vast and fair,
Then could she all her tale relate
  To that sweet lady dwelling there.
But all her little courage fled :
With fainting steps she homeward sped.

XXXVII

First slowly, then with swifter pace,
  She outran terror at her heels,
As if to win with Death the race,
  Whose shroud now brushing by she feels.
She starts at every rugged bank,
For with the sun her spirit sank.

XXXVIII

The orb, yet vast beyond the height,
  Had set more early in the wood ;
But o'er the trees the lingering light
  Spread floating in a rosy flood.
The birds sank one by one to rest,
As pale and paler grew the west.

XXXIX

She spied her cot, O vision sweet!
  A rushlight through the lattice flamed,
And threw its radiance at her feet,
  As it the grudging twilight shamed.
Through diamond panes a glimpse to catch,
She held her finger on the latch.

XL

No sound, no breath she heard above,
  Where grandsire in the garret lay.
But one was there whose looks of love,
  'Poor little orphan,' seemed to say.
She knew the chaplain's kindly face;
The bearer of the lady's grace.

XLI

'Where hast thou been, my darling maid?
  Reply to one who likes thee well.'
'To fetch the raven home,' she said;
  'And him my grandsire's wants to tell.
I stood beneath the raven-tree
And found no bird to succour me.'

THE LILY OF THE VALLEY

'Why call the raven to thy door,
  Thy little heart's distress to share?'
'Because,' said she, 'the sire is poor,
  And has not earned his daily fare.
All father's work he leaves undone,
And says I soon shall be alone.'

'To kiss thee, child, he would have stayed,
  For oft he called thee to his side.
Where didst thou wander, little maid?'
  'I went across the world so wide.
I looked at heaven and saw its scope,
Taught by my mother there was hope.

'I looked for mother in the sky :
  She taught me there my wants to tell;
I looked for father standing by,
  For both among the happy dwell;
I cried to them with heart of care,
Can God the prophet's raven spare?

THE LILY OF THE VALLEY

XLV

'Then I came nigh a stately pile,
  Where those who ask seek not in vain.
I looked, and saw a human smile,
  And thought a lady looked again.
Through windows I beheld her face,
As she looked from her heavenly place.

XLVI

'And then I to the lady said,
  "Can God the prophet's raven spare?
For grandsire lies upon his bed,
  And has not earned his daily fare.
My father's work he leaves undone,
And says I soon shall be alone."'

XLVII

'Thou art not all alone, my child;
  Thy griefs that righteous lady hears:
She loves a spirit undefiled;
  Her heart is open to thy tears.
Thy father's work at last is done,
And thou shalt never be alone.'

THE LOVER'S DAY

I

GORSE-PLAINS that flower their gold into the streams
  Beneath the opal blossoms of the sky ;
Sea-floods that weave their blue and purple seams ;
  White sails that lift the billows as they fly :
  Not these in their abounding rapture vie
With love's diviner dreams.

II

Those lovers tire not when the sun is pale ;
  No statelier awning than a bristled tree
With branches cedared by the salten gale,
  Stretched back, as if with wings that cannot flee :
  They linger, and the sun departs by sea ;
He spreads his crimson sail.

III

They watch him as he piles his busy deck
    With golden treasure ; as his sail expands ;
They see him sink ; they gaze upon the wreck
    Through the still twilight of the silvery sands.
    One cloud is left to the deserted lands :
The blue-set moon's cold fleck.

IV

They linger though the pageant hath gone by,
    The opal cloud is lit o'er sea and plain ;
The moon is full of one day's memory,
    And tells the tale of Nature o'er again,
    Its glory mingled in the soul's refrain
Under that lover's sky.

THE DEADLY NIGHTSHADE

I

There was a haunt, it does not change,
  Not while the fiend its path invades;
But he who did its alleys range
  Has willed his penance to its shades.
There still the nightshade breathes its pest
On fallen spirits not at rest.

II

It is the haunt it was of yore,
  A den where thieves and harlots creep,
Where Nature's voice is heard no more,
  Where guilt-stained men night-vigil keep,
And crimes like months afresh appear,—
Ere one runs out, another near.

III

A haunt where all in common share
   The sleepless hour, the murderous toil ;
Where Death on all has set his stare,
   To drag them forth, to grasp their spoil :
Between their gallows and their den,
A hardening sight for other men.

IV

This is the charnel that doth hide
   A frantic woman who at play
Has lost her wealth of virgin pride,
   And reckless games her soul away ;
Whose scarlet rags, deep-dyed, replace
The blushes of her maiden face.

V

A mother's bitter hour sets in ;
   Wrecked on her breast the infant lies,
As if to perish for its sin,
   There set adrift from human ties
Till its ear-piercing scream prevail
And sullen pity hush the wail.

VI

Where only shadows rise and set,
  And love at morn awaketh not,
This child of woe his being met,
  To share a loveless parent's lot,
And at his birth his sentence meet
Before a mother's judgment-seat.

VII

The mother moaning in the gloom
  Laughed when a peaceful breath he drew,
Too conscious of his early doom.
  On wounded wings the tidings flew,
On bosoms pitiless they fell:
'A child of heaven was born in hell!'

VIII

His place of birth the skies deplored,
  No trees, no brooks, no meadows seen;
And still his heart those skies adored
  Before he saw the fields were green.
Born amid broils, in squalor bred,
His soul knew not to where it sped.

D

IX

The child is taught through many a blow
　To shed with sobs the beggar's tear,
Reared as a prodigy of woe
　That gentle women pay to hear.
And many listened and bestowed;
For younger tears had never flowed.

X

Held at his mother's hand, he hung
　A broken spray with misery's drip;
And often to the ground he clung,
　His passion bursting at his lip.
And still she dragged him o'er the stones,
Though tender was he to the bones.

XI

Her eyes of prey like fangs were laid
　On all who gave a hurried look.
And while she whined for kindly aid,
　She hid away the coin she took,
When suddenly she begged no more
And rushed within a slamming door.

XII

With nostrils spread, and eyes aflame,
  Before the shrine of death she stands,
The infant by her, sick and lame,
  The lava trembling in her hands.
She drinks it with a vengeful frown ;
She feels the fiend of sorrow drown.

XIII

Now in a prison left to rage,
  She thirsts, she burns with vain desire
Her deadly sickness to assuage,
  To quench its fiery pang in fire.
With what a mother sent to dwell,
This child of heaven reared up in hell !

XIV

Not far away from infancy—
  Through weary time a single stage,
The livelong years had hustled by
  But left him still of tender age,
When from his mother's reach he fled,
Outside the doors to make his bed.

XV

Where odours wander, dank and foul,
   Through crowded streets and alleys lone,
By day and night his footsteps prowl;
   His wants, not many, asked by none:
The roads were new he hourly crossed,
Yet was his way not wholly lost.

XVI

When hunger like a conscience cries,
   He asks the needy to bestow,
Afraid to raise his drooping eyes
   Except to those who famine know;
Such he believes their crust will break,
And share with him for pity's sake.

XVII

Hopeful, he glides into a den
   Up whose dusk path a shudder flew,
And asks of sick, half-famished men
   Whose strength no plenty could renew.
Yet with what startling oaths they rave
And bid him run his neck to save!

XVIII

Still to the poor is his appeal,
  And they his mild entreaty spurn :
Some whisper, Be a man and steal ;
  Some bid him to the gallows turn.
Child-like he credits all he hears,
And rests his troubled heart in tears.

XIX

He rests,—but oft starts up in fear ;
  His mother's driving shadow breaks
Upon his slumber unaware,
  And sleep's too light repast awakes
Where dreams the festive board have spread
And turned his sorrow into bread.

XX

Hope, 'mid those shapes of famine sent,
  Smiles on him ;—she is Childhood's bride !
The mother's image, o'er him bent,
  Cannot the angel wholly hide,—
Not when her halo o'er him plays,
And all but hunger's pang allays.

XXI

How did he long for once to taste
    Of the forbidden food whose smell
From cellar gratings ran to waste !
    Gusts that the passing crowd repel.
As when a rose some maid regales,
The grateful vapour he inhales.

XXII

Less favoured than the dog outside,
    He lingers by some savoury mass ;
He watches mouths that open wide,
    And sees them eating through the glass.
Oft his own lips he opes and shuts,
And sympathy his fancy gluts.

XXIII

So, oft a-hungered has he stood,
    And yarn of fasting fancy spun,
As wistfully he watched the food,
    With one foot out prepared to run,
In vague misgiving of his right
To revel in the dainty sight.

XXIV

Harmless, yet to the base akin,
    He feels a blot no eye could see,
And drags his rags about his skin
    To hide from view his pedigree.
He deems himself a thief by birth,
An alien on the teeming earth.

XXV

He begs not, but as in a trance
    Admires the gay and wealthy throng;
But if the curious on him glance,
    He is abashed and slinks along;
He cares no more, the spell once broke,
Scenes of false plenty to invoke.

XXVI

The man of charity beholds
    His vagrant looks with pent-up grief;
He stops, reproves; he gently scolds,
    But fails to give the child relief;
'So sad,' he says, 'to see them thrive
Who on another's earnings live.'

XXVII

Then comes the child, this ill-sown seed,
    To sweep the purlieus and the wynds,
But few bethink them of his need,
    And scanty is the help he finds.
At times he walks upon his head :
A form of prayer for daily bread.

XXVIII

Now seem his days for sorrow made !
    He hears that men on Sunday pray ;
A world's proud secret on parade
    To him appears the Sabbath-day.
All have asked heaven to take their cares,
But hunger says for him his prayers.

XXIX

Some words have reached him such as jar
    On sinners' ears and seem devout ;
They are but as a light from far,
    They come from heaven and soon die out,
Too weak as yet to turn a spell
Wove in the alphabet of hell.

FLOWERS ON THE BANK

I

Flowers on the bank,—we pass and call them gay :
  The primroses throw pictures to the mind,
  The buttercups lag dazzlingly behind,
And daisy-friends we spy but do not say
  A word of joy ;—thoughts of them follow not,
  And soon are they forgot.

II

What care we for wildflowers except their name ?
  Bright maidens at the sight in rapture start,
  Which, as our smiles say, comes not from the
    heart :
Flowers dance not, sing not, all their ways are tame ;
  They love not, neither love in us inspire ;
  Nor blush when we admire.

III

Yet stay, the fingers of that panting child
  Have culled for us the choice ones,—many a
    gem,—
  Have set their lovely colours stem to stem
In her fond hands they are not tame or wild,
  Nestled in fringy fern so changed appears
  The little gift she bears!

IV

She gives herself, and she can dance and sing,
  And she can love inspire and blush at praise;
  The flowers are part of her, have caught her
    ways;
She gives herself who gives so sweet a thing.
  And she is gone, with other thoughts than ours
  Gathering fresh love and flowers.

THE BLIND BOY

I

In dark ascent the pine-clad hills
  Repose on heaven their rocky crest.
Lit by the flash of falling rills
  That in the valley-shadow rest,
Chafing in rainbow-spray that finds
Its sunshine in the gusty winds.

II

Clouds folded round the topmost peaks
  Shut out the gorges from the sun :
'Tis mid-day ere the early streaks
  Of sunshine down the valley run ;
But where the opening cliffs expand,
The early sea-light breaks on land.

III

Before the sun, like golden shields,
   The clouds a lustre shed around;
Wild shadows gambol o'er the fields;
   Tame shadows stretch upon the ground.
Towards noon the great rock-shadow moves,
And takes slow leave of all it loves.

IV

The beam-shot clouds dissolve apace;
   Stray shades that linger like a scroll,
Draw nearer to their craggy base,
   And in clefts and caverns roll;
The light falls down the rocky piles;
The vale a lake of glory smiles.

V

There dwell two orphans: Heaven ordains
   The sister's eyes shall live in light:
Her brother in the shade remains
   When morning bursts upon her sight.
Sister and brother, far and wide
As one they wander side by side.

VI

When to the shore through woods and fields
  The brother has a wish to stray,
The sister takes the hand he yields;
  She by fond habit leads the way.
Skipping along, oft face to face,
Her hand directs his timid pace.

VII

The plains that strike the grey-white line
  Where earth's dim curve in distance fades;
The streams that near the dwelling shine;
  The quiet meads; the rustling glades;
The sand-dunes waiting on the shore,
The sister's eyes for him explore.

VIII

'Tis all his own, but her loved hand,
  Her gentle voice, her sayings dear,
Are choicer gifts than all the land
  That he inherits far and near,
For all his light is in her mind,—
The path he loses she can find.

IX

At early morn, embraced by her,
 He sits within the shadow's dip
To list to his sweet minister,
 And paint his visions from her lip.
He sees the waters, earth, and skies
Only through her enchanted eyes.

X

Her eyes are bright, his now are blind ;
 All he once saw has passed away,
But her fond visions fill his mind,
 And there disclose the dawn of day.
Her morning breaks upon his night,
Enlivened by her spirit's light.

XI

She tells him how the mountains swell,
 How rocks and forests touch the skies ;
He tells her how the shadows dwell
 In purple dimness on his eyes,
Whose tremulous orbs the while he lifts,
As round his smile their spirit drifts.

XII

More close around his heart to wind,
  She shuts her eyes in childish glee,
'To share,' she says, 'his peace of mind;
  To sit beneath his shadow-tree.'
So, half in play, the sister tries
To find his soul within her eyes.

XIII

His hand in hers, she walks along
  And leads him by the river's brink;
She stays to catch the water's song,
  Closing her eyes with him to think.
His ear, more watchful than her own,
Had caught the ocean's distant moan.

XIV

'The river's flow is bright and clear,'
  The blind boy said, 'and were it dark
We should no less its music hear:
  Sings not at eventide the lark?
Still when the ripples pause, they fade
Upon my spirit like a shade.'

XV

'Yet, brother, when the river stops
    And in the quiet bay is hushed,
E'en though its gentle murmur drops,
    'Tis bright as when by us it rushed;
Not like a shade, when heard no more,
Except beneath the wooded shore.'

XVI

Now the resounding beach, wave-swept,
    Greets them; now silence softly bears
The likeness of the wave that leapt
    Unseen, and broke upon their ears.
'Dear sister, tell me once again
The wonders of the sea's domain!'

XVII

Down the moist sands she guides his way,
    And gazes on the lonesome shores,
Where desultory waves at play,
    Enthral her looks ere she explores
The far-off deep; ere those quick eyes
Rove o'er the waters, cliffs, and skies.

XVIII

'The farthest seas bend as a bow
　Into the light, o'er-arching sky;
There, curdled breakers row on row
　With scarce a motion, distant lie;
Or if one vanish from the rest,
It shows again its snowy crest.

XIX

'But nearer, midway toward the sands,
　I see long lines of billows creep;
One stops and into froth expands,
　Then fades away upon the deep;
Close to the shore the waves contend,
And shouting reach the journey's end.'

XX

While her bright tones upon him broke
　The curtain from his soul was drawn;
His spirit quickened as she spoke,—
　Then flashed as at a sudden dawn,
With visions of a world once known,
That for the moment seemed his own.

E

XXI

'O tell me of the changing sky,
   Sunless once more!'   ''Neath lovely blue,'
The sister says, 'the clouds float by,
   Of orange, white, and inky hue.
The shifting waves that cannot rest
Are 'neath the gusty breezes pressed.

XXII

'A cloud is loosened from the sun;
   The sea's sky-blue now skims the green,
Chasing the billows as they run
   And drip their foam in troughs between.
Oh, could you see them as they roar,
Scooping away the glistening shore!'

XXIII

'The waves,' he said, 'before me fall,
   And memories of a long-lost light
From far-off mornings on me call,
   And what I hear comes into sight.
The beauteous skies flash back again,
But, ah! the light will not remain!'

XXIV

Awhile he pauses ; as he stops,
  Her little hand the sister moves
And pebbles on the water drops,
  As it runs up the sandy grooves,
Or to her ear a shell applies,
With parted lips and dreaming eyes.

XXV

'That noise !' said he, with lifted hand.
  'The sea-gull's scream and flapping wings,
Before the wind it flies to land,
  And omens of a tempest brings.'
She tells him how the sea-bird pale
Whirls wildly on the coming gale.

XXVI

'And is the sea alone ? Even now
  I hear faint mutterings,—not the waves';
It seems a murmur sweeping low
  And hurrying through the distant caves.
I hear again that smothered tone,
As if the sea were not alone.'

XXVII

'Heaven slopes o'er us on every side,
  And shuts us from the distant land.
The waters only here abide,
  And we who sit upon the sand.
A porpoise revels in the spray,
And purple vapours veil the bay.

XXVIII

'Come, hasten,' cries she, 'to the woods
  Where twisted boughs are thickly set,
For soon the rain must fall in floods :
  Here is no shelter from the wet.
While like a sea the sky upheaves,
We'll watch beneath the matted leaves.'

XXIX

'Stay, sister !   Listen to that sound ;—
  It thunders—does the flash appear?'
'It lightens now, and, whirling round,
  The gull dips low, as if in fear.'
The boy now turns his floating eyes,
Though not the way the sea-bird flies.

THE BLIND BOY

'The wind is balmy on my cheek,
    But now I feel the rain-drop plash.
Let us,' he said, 'the woodland seek,
    And hear it on the foliage dash.
On the ground-ivy we shall tread,
And through the grove its perfume spread.'

XXXI

And so they prattle as they leave
    The sandy beach, in pensive mood,
His ear turned to the billow's heave,
    Her vision leaning on the wood,
While, as the honeysuckle clings,
About his neck her arm she flings.

Better than she the blind boy hears
    The whispers of the patient shore,
While yet the wave its crest uprears
    To break once more,—and evermore.
Better than she the blind boy feels
The simple pictures she reveals.

XXXIII

Clapping her hands, she spies above
   Rich elms, the turrets grey and old,—
But love of home was only love
   When to her darling brother told.
Thus ever to his soul replies
The infant passion of her eyes.

XXXIV

While they return, the dwelling near,
   One word must yet the sister say.
She lifts her voice: 'O brother dear,
   If good my eyes have been to-day,
Kiss them for every new delight
That kindles in your spirit's sight!'

XXXV

Deep in his eyes the love-lights strove;
   He clasped her in a close embrace:—
With lips that shook with grateful love
   He kissed her eyes—he kissed her face—
He wept upon that tender brow;
'Dearest, the darkness leaves me now!

XXXVI

'I view all beauty through your eyes;
  I see within, you see outside.
Your love has raised me to the skies,—
  Once narrow,—lofty now and wide,
And not, as once, of sombre hue;
For I can dream the dark to blue.

XXXVII

'The upward-toiling hill; the stream;
  The valley; the wide ocean's sweep;
All take the colours of a dream,—
  The glories of the land of sleep.
You are my soul, my eyes, my sight;
'Tis dark no more, you are my light.'

WHEN I THINK OF THEE, BROTHER

I

WHEN I think of thee, brother,
  Is my heart not all thine?
Yet the face of another
  Seems bending o'er mine.
I call thee by name, yet a name not thy own
Has whispered already its dear undertone.

II

When I think thine eyes greet me,
  Their sweet flash of blue
Brings another's to meet me
  Of somberer hue;
And ever before me they seem to remain,
Though my heart but repines to behold thee
    again.

III

When I list, and would hear thee
  Once more in our home,
And thy voice appears near me,
  Another's has come.
I dream of thee only, for thee only sigh,
Yet thy image forsakes me; another's is nigh.

IV

When thy fond smiles come o'er me,
  As in moments now flown,
There riseth before me
  A look not thy own:
'Tis thee I recall to my mind, O my brother!
Yet ever with thine comes the gaze of another.

ECCE HOMO !

I

HE strikes his staff to find his way,
He feels but may not see the day.
The warm sun floods his sightless eyes
That tremble in answer to the skies:
Yet oft he stays as if to look
    At memories of the scenes of yore,—
    The vine and fig-tree at his door,
The pleasant places by the brook.

II

The voice within him sighs aloud,
When murmurs of a moving crowd
Fall on his ear; he breathes the dust
But, with a blind man's sturdy trust,

He grasps his staff, and oft he cries,
'Who cometh here?'   A voice replies,
' O blind man, turn thy step aside,
'Tis Christ!'

III

The name rings in his ears :
With flashing hopes and ashen fears,
     There stands he breathless, startling all.
Some stop, some into ranks divide,
     Their arms outspreading lest he fall.
He drops his staff, throws out his hands,
     His fingers are creeping like things that see :
'Mid all the multitude he stands
     And shouts, ' Have mercy, Lord, on me !'
His shaking beard, his tottering frame,
     His eye-balls in their sockets turning,
His lips delirious with that name,—
     O'er his blind face a look is burning
Of dreadful greed, with mouth agape,
Crazed for some good that may escape.
' Take my hand, some one ; let me feel
His raiment only ; it may heal.'

IV

Christ heard the blind man's cry, and grieved
Because a soul in darkness heaved.
　　He said, 'What seekest thou of Me?'
But in that presence came a fear :
The man held earthly blessings dear,
Yet more than all was heavenly light.
'Lord, that I may receive my sight,—
　　That I may my Redeemer see!'
Christ loved him and his anguish soothed.
He took his hand, He gently smoothed
The seams upon his wrinkled brow :
'Tell Me what thou beholdest now.'
'Men, dim as shaking trees, I see :
O Lord, I crave to look on Thee!'

V

Then said the Saviour, 'Look afar.'
　　The blind man raised his dazèd eyes.
'I see, Lord, above Thee a new-risen star,—
　　And beneath it a babe in a manger lies.
　　Hoary men, kneeling, their gifts prefer :
　　Frankincense, gold, and sacred myrrh.

Now a mother, a father, a babe softly sleeping
  By waters that dream where the lotus bloom
    reigns ;
Shadows of evening over them creeping ;
  The broad moon breaking o'er palm-bearing
    plains,
Where the ibis croaks and the jackal cries,
And pyramids point to the purpling skies.'

VI

  He pauses, still he looks afar.
  He still beholds the guiding star,
  And dreamlight of a sacred river
  O'er his lone eyes seems still to quiver.
Sudden, as if the distant air
  Stripped the blue curtain from the skies,
He sees prophetic nature bare,—
  When, as with far-off voice, he cries—
'Lo ! a face to heaven in agony gleaming,
  Stained of sorrow, but soil-less of sin,
Sweat that is blood breaking and streaming
  From brows that are throbbing of anguish
    within,—

Praying for those that do strip Him and scourge
    Him
  As a cross on His quivering shoulders they place.
'Neath its burden He sinks while they mock Him,
    they urge Him,
    They crown Him with thorns, they spit in His
     face.
They are lifting Him, bruising Him, piercing Him,
    nailing Him
  To the cross, that is dyed in a crimson flood.
See, the sun hides his head, see the vapour en-
    veiling him,
Hark, the earth and the skies in the darkness
    bewailing Him
  Who dieth for those that are shedding His blood.'

VII

He starts, a hand is on his brow.
  He looks at Christ in meek surprise,
  Tears gather in his new-lit eyes ;
  ''Tis He, the crucified !' he cries :
' Yes, I behold the Saviour now !'
  The adoring people kneel around ;
  The healed one sinks on the hallowed ground,

Then goes his way in silence and in awe;
  For his unsullied eyes had seen
  The sight that from the first had been,
The sight that nature like a prophet saw.

THE SNAKE CHARMER

I

THE forest rears on lifted arms
   Its leafy dome whence verdurous light
Shakes through the shady depths and warms
   Proud trunk and stealthy parasite,
There where those cruel coils enclasp
The trees they strangle in their grasp.

II

An old man creeps from out the woods,
   Breaking the vine's entangling spell;
He thrids the jungle's solitudes
   O'er bamboos rotting where they fell;
Slow down the tiger's path he wends
Where at the pool the jungle ends.

III

No moss-greened alley tells the trace
  Of his lone step, no sound is stirred,
Even when his tawny hands displace
  The boughs, that backward sweep unheard :
His way as noiseless as the trail
Of the swift snake and pilgrim snail.

IV

The old snake-charmer,—once he played
  Soft music for the serpent's ear,
But now his cunning hand is stayed ;
  He knows the hour of death is near.
And all that live in brake and bough,
All know the brand is on his brow.

V

Yet where his soul is he must go :
  He crawls along from tree to tree.
The old snake-charmer, doth he know
  If snake or beast of prey he be ?
Bewildered at the pool he lies
And sees as through a serpent's eyes.

F

VI

Weeds wove with white-flowered lily crops
   Drink of the pool, and serpents hie
To the thin brink as noonday drops,
   And in the froth-daubed rushes lie.
There rests he now with fastened breath
'Neath a kind sun to bask in death.

VII

The pool is bright with glossy dyes
   And cast-up bubbles of decay :
A green death-leaven overlies
   Its mottled scum, where shadows play
As the snake's hollow coil, fresh shed,
Rolls in the wind across its bed.

VIII

No more the wily note is heard
   From his full flute—the riving air
That tames the snake, decoys the bird,
   Worries the she-wolf from her lair.
Fain would he bid its parting breath
Drown in his ears the voice of death.

IX

Still doth his soul's vague longing skim
   The pool beloved : he hears the hiss
That siffles at the sedgy rim,
   Recalling days of former bliss,
And the death-drops, that fall in showers,
Seem honied dews from shady flowers.

X

There is a rustle of the breeze
   And twitter of the singing bird ;
He snatches at the melodies
   And his faint lips again are stirred :
The olden sounds are in his ears ;
But still the snake its crest uprears.

XI

His eyes are swimming in the mist
   That films the earth like serpent's breath ;
And now—as if a serpent hissed—
   The husky whisperings of Death
Fill ear and brain—he looks around—
Serpents seem matted o'er the ground.

XII

Soon visions of past joys bewitch
 His crafty soul ; his hands would set
Death's snare, while now his fingers twitch
 At tasselled reed as 'twere his net.
But his thin lips no longer fill
The woods with song ; his flute is still.

XIII

Those lips still quaver to the flute,
 But fast the life-tide ebbs away ;
Those lips now quaver and are mute,
 But nature throbs in breathless play :
Birds are in open song, the snakes
Are watching in the silent brakes.

XIV

In sudden fear of snares unseen
 The birds like crimson sunset swarm,
All gold and purple, red and green,
 And seek each other for the charm.
Lizards dart up the feathery trees
Like shadows of a rainbow breeze.

THE SNAKE CHARMER

XV

The wildered birds again have rushed
　Into the charm,—it is the hour
When the shrill forest-note is hushed,
　And they obey the serpent's power,—
Drawn to its gaze with troubled whirr,
As by the thread of falconer.

XVI

As 'twere to feed, on slanting wings
　They drop within the serpent's glare :
Eyes flashing fire in burning rings
　Which spread into the dazzled air ;
They flutter in the glittering coils ;
The charmer dreads the serpent's toils.

XVII

While Music swims away in death
　Man's spell is passing to his slaves :
The snake feeds on the charmer's breath,
　The vulture screams, the parrot raves,
The lone hyena laughs and howls,
The tiger from the jungle growls.

XVIII

Then mounts the eagle—flame-flecked folds
  Belt its proud plumes; a feather falls:
He hears the death-cry, he beholds
  The king-bird in the serpent's thralls,
He looks with terror on the feud,—
And the sun shines through dripping blood.

XIX

The deadly spell a moment gone—
  Birds, from a distant Paradise,
Strike the winged signal and have flown,
  Trailing rich hues through azure skies:
The serpent falls; like demon wings
The far-out branching cedar swings.

XX

The wood swims round; the pool and skies
  Have met; the death-drops down that cheek
Fall faster; for the serpent's eyes
  Grow human, and the charmer's seek.
A gaze like man's directs the dart
Which now is buried at his heart.

XXI

The monarch of the world is cold :
   The charm he bore has passed away :
The serpent gathers up its fold
   To wind about its human prey.
The red mouth darts a dizzy sting,
And clenches the eternal ring.

PYTHAGORAS

I

'Twas not the hour of death the Master feared :
    He oft had died before, his soul had passed
Through many moulds, as each new cycle neared
    Hoping the Golden Day had come at last.

II

But like a giant 'neath the weight of age
    Hope was bowed down, and oft had ceased to see
Among the spheres the looked for heritage
    Where rest the pure from earth's illusions free.

III

Whither doth this metempsychosis tend ?
    Doubt stirs the heavy question in his breast.
All that begins is toiling towards its end ;
    Oblivion hath for all its day of rest.

IV

And when a universe of death absorbs
    Into its hungry vortex all that is :
The compact colonies of settled orbs,
    The untamed meteors of the free abyss ;

V

And when, at length, the lamp of day is spent,
    And the charred air of night supplants the skies,
What were the soul without its tenement,—
    Without these feeling hands, these seeing eyes ?

VI

Even the blest dawn he once had hoped to find
    May rise while he in darkness dwells below ;
Yes, all may fail him now ; the troubled mind
    May end at last, and not its ending know.

VII

Such were his thoughts, and while his death hour
    grew
    They pressed into his heart such poignant pangs
As even the lordliest intellect subdue
    When life, yet wavering, in the balance hangs.

VIII

'Tis past : A cycle's lustres have run out,
  And his unquickened soul in ashes sleeps,
Perturbed no longer by the wasting doubt,
  Weak as a babe ere in the womb it leaps ;

IX

Still as a vessel stranded by the tide
  In shallows whereunto no waters drift,
Looming at anchor on its mouldering side
  That neither winds disturb nor billows lift.

X

Yet throes half-stir the drowsings of the grave,
  As when one turns in sleep with heavy sense
That what suspended being he may have
  Is better, yet awhile, with Providence.

XI

But all is like the passing of a breath.
  No eager promptings snatch the loosened thread
Wherein is meshed the memory of death :
  He knows himself, but not that he is dead.

XII

Another cycle bears the cumbrous night
  Unbroken, save as funeral clouds may roll
And for a moment cross the path of light :
  So shines the ethereal darkness of his soul.

XIII

Still through these mists of death the cycles shone,—
  His soul benumbed, in utter silence hushed,
Advancing time-like through oblivion,
  And pace for pace with all that o'er him rushed,—

XIV

When to his grave a sense of nature came,
  But with no conscious meaning or surprise :
'Twas the old flutter of the dying flame,
  Tremulousness of being without eyes.

XV

At last a voice, familiar as to seem
  His own, heard in his sleep and heeded not,
Broke through the patient whisper of his dream,
  Remembered but to be as soon forgot.

XVI

It presages some mighty morrow near
  When his long baffled soul once more shall rise :
The muffled cycles fall upon his ear,
  And his dust flutters with the centuries.

XVII

Awake, Pythagoras, it seems to say,—
  The looked-for morn is breaking o'er the earth :
It grows, it brightens to the perfect day ;
  Behold man's resurrectionary birth !

XVIII

His thoughts take shape, his pent-up senses move,
  His soul looks out from that abysmal sleep.
Lo ! shadows of the living world above
  Before his eyes in dreamy pageant sweep.

XIX

And in the midst there shone a god-like youth,
  Who on his brow the Crown of Sorrow wore,
And there was meekness, innocence, and truth ;—
  Eidolon of his highest hope of yore.

XX

Hath it then come at last, the world of peace?
  Hath he awakened to that ampler life
Where hate and lust of blood shall ever cease,
  And all the bitter days of human strife?

XXI

The world is hushed: must then the cycles end
  That ever deepen his immortal tomb?
The wondrous ladder must he re-ascend
  To truths revolving round a virgin womb?

XXII

Even so it seems when, hark! the upper air
  Rings to the battle's rage—the soldier's tread
Echoes above his tomb!   In dark despair
  He turns his face unto the silent dead.

XXIII

The Master sleeps—the ages onward roll—
  O twice nine stormy cycles since o'erpast!
Bore they through eddying lives and deaths a soul
  Still dreaming towards its Golden Day at last?

XXIV

The heavens are as they were, the sun, unworn,
  Seems on the blue of yesterday to rest,
And drops below; but when shall come the morn
  He dreamt of, when shall break that morrow
    blest?

THE FIRST SAVED

I

Lucilla lives in yon half-hidden star
  Bowered in a dreamy, soft-skied, watery vale,
Where angels gather from bright worlds afar,
  To see her face, and listen to her tale.

II

As if all sunset revelled in the air,
  The rosy clouds float o'er her paradise,—
Home of the once lone daughter of despair
  Who prayed through tears with ever downcast
  eyes.

III

The lucent hills pant in the azure beams,
  Behind empurpled steeps that blend below
With trembling woods and crystal-bearing streams,
  And in the sky-paved water-mirrors glow.

IV

As rising stars entangle in their spheres
   All the blue ether round, her look of thought
Hangs in heaven's light, where her sad life appears
   A sunless vision in new sunshine wrought.

V

There doth she stand, bliss-stricken as by fear.
   On one soft hand she rests her chin and cheek,
Paling with rapture ere the blush appear ;
   And lips in tremors whisper that would speak.

VI

' Yes, I am here, and Heaven is undefiled !
   This sinless face and these all-loving eyes
God gave me when I was a little child,
   Because I was to be in Paradise.

VII

' I heard a voice and slavery's loosened bond
   Fell from my soul, awaking me to die ;
I looked into death's mirror and beyond
   I saw these halls of immortality.

VIII

' My wounded heart lay in this bosom dead
   Ere it had loved—yet oft as I did pray
That these wan hands might labour for their bread,
   Hope only came to prayer but did not stay.

IX

' Sin compassed me, it was my deadly fate ;
   Yet lovely visions in the darkness came,
And I fled trembling to the Temple's gate
   But durst not cross the threshold for my shame.

X

' While on the Temple's steps I sat in tears,
   One came and spoke : I gazed and I adored !
Then did a voice that only woman hears
   Whisper within : I listened, self-abhorred.

XI

' 'Twas He whose image visited my sleep.
   But still He spake to me in words that gave
A world, and had soul-echoes clear and deep
   Which widened ever like the circling wave.

XII

'His image grew before my wondering mind—
  His, 'mid whose many griefs my life began.
Enrapt I gazed, until my eyes were blind,
  On Him who in His pity dies for man.

XIII

'When the blest vision ceased, my eyes would droop
  And in great dreams that holy Being meet;
Then would He clothe me, lowly would He stoop,
  And with His hands anoint my weary feet.

XIV

'Thenceforth He was the rock that safely drew
  My heart to shelter, as the gentle shore
Receives the broken wave : to Him it flew
  And the lulled sorrow beat on me no more.

XV

'Then o'er me flowed that stream of heavenly grace
  Which all my infant innocence restored :
From that glad hour has rested on my face
  This happy gaze of one who has adored.

XVI

'The living Saviour had my heart enthralled!
  I saw His face, in His blessed footsteps moved;
And in my dreams His holy word recalled;
  I knew not who He was: I only loved.

XVII

'Then did I but remember things to come,
  The reveries of pure delights above;
Yes, to this blissful height my passion clomb,
  And sin was silenced in the hush of love.

XVIII

'In that o'ershadowing trance till death I lay:
  Peace weighed upon me like the Saviour's kiss.
Towards the beloved my eyes would fondly stray
  In sleeping rapture and awaking bliss.

XIX

'Death with dis-shadowed hand had come betimes,
  And bore my grave into the open skies.
And then I hearkened to the heavenly chimes
  That cheered my soul's ascent to Paradise.

XX

'My end seemed consummated in the clouds :
 There with the purple morn my slumber broke ;
But tempting spirits hovered round in crowds
 And gathered like a storm as I awoke.

XXI

' Upon the Temple's highest pinnacle
 The Saviour stood in glory like the sun.
The rapture of my soul was at the full :
 Eternal life had unawares begun.

XXII

' He from that holy height upon me gazed ;
 The angels in His glorious presence trod :
With outstretched wings I rushed to them amazed
 And flew into the open arms of God.'

REMINISCENCE

1

So you would leave me, little Rose ?
  Dear child, with all your mother's ways ;
  That look she had in girlish days,
The look that with your beauty grows.

II

Oft when you bring her to my mind,
  Before my heart has time for pain,
  In you she seems to live again,
As though no sorrow were behind.

III

And when that happy, trustful gaze
  Meets him you love, yet more I see
  Your mother as she looked at me :
It is her own dear, watchful face.

IV

And when he takes your hand in his,
   There flits across your lips and eyes
   Her own pleased smile of half surprise :
It seems not like departed bliss.

V

Ah ! what a heart-locked memory stirs—
   I look, 'tis she, and you are gone !
   Yes, though so many springs have flown,
Her peace remains, our love is hers.

VI

She sees your arms my neck enclose ;
   She sees your lips upon my brow.
   No truer hour of love than now
Awaits your heart, my happy Rose !

VII

How they come back those days of old !
   And now that 'tis your wedding-eve,
   Now that for other scenes you leave,
One happy legend shall be told,—

VIII

Told in this home, this sunny vale
   That for long years has been our own,
   Sacred in days that long have gone
To many another lover's tale.

IX

It was an hour like this, the sun
   Was sinking, yet had far to go:
   The richness of his overflow
Down river, wood, and pasture shone.

X

Two lovers in this porch had met
   Where often they had met in play:
   'Twas on this memorable day—
As though that sun had never set.

XI

These grey-mossed tiles still 'neath it scorch;
   The glare and shade still side by side
   Aslant the mullioned casements glide
From yon old gable to the porch.

XII

A youth has hurried from these walls—
  He stops, as in a day-dream stands:
  His shadow with fast-folded hands
As from yon stone sun-dial falls.

XIII

His eyes are full of one loved face
  Sunk pallid in her fingers cleft;
  The long-loved one who just had left
In timid haste his wild embrace.

XIV

The love that with her childhood grew
  Had still to her unruffled clung;
  Engaging, playful, ever young,—
And without change was ever new.

XV

Not its glad pastimes she disowns:
  He drew her to a higher love;
  But while the pale emotion strove
She fled from his impassioned tones.

XVI

Transparent isles of rushes bind
 The rivers light with bars of green
 That catch the water's blue between,
To where it darkens in the wind.

XVII

There lies his boat, and now the sun,
 Still going westward with the stream,
 Appears to tow him on his dream
As they advance in unison.

XVIII

Along the white and yellow meads,
 Which buttercup and daisy share,
 The crowding cattle idly stare
As he winds through the matted reeds.

XIX

But her loved image fills his mind,
 And, ever gazing at him, screens
 His eyes from those long-happy scenes,
As he drifts by them, nature-blind.

XX

The white-flowered weed whose tresses float,
　　Combed by the stream and water-waved,
　　Seems her bright hair in crystal laved,
Struggling to overtake his boat.

XXI

His sculls drip o'er the glossy wash:
　　The ripple of the mellow tide
　　He scarce feels o'er their edges glide;
He lists not for the thrilling plash,

XXII

But thinks, when last the tide he clove,
　　How bank-side elms before him flew,
　　And quiet lay the distant view
Of woodland hill where dwelt his love.

XXIII

His memory holds it as the stream
　　Holds all the shining summer round:
　　The sky, the woods, the very sound
Ot cuckoos chanting in a dream.

XXIV

And how she loved the grey old bridge !
  Those arches mirrored deep below,
  That meet the pillars row to row,
Quivering from their ruffled ridge—

XXV

Three tunnels open to the skies !
  The tasselled mosses as they float,
  Now still, now heaving with the boat
That passes while the vision flies.

XXVI

As melt, with all the watery heaven,
  Those arches hanging o'er a sky—
  So in the quiet of a sigh
The yearnings of his soul seemed riven.

XXVII

The far-off boom of yonder weir
  Now rushes down the narrowed day :
  Like sirens battling with the spray,
Once came its music to her ear.

XXVIII

The sun now trembles like a ball
    Heaven-forged and glittering in its blast;
    A pale green halo round him cast—
Half quenched behind the waterfall.

XXIX

White streaks are creeping through the shade;
    The moon climbs up the poplar trees:
    But a loved form of light he sees,
As if her spirit walked the glade.

XXX

Well might it be, as since hath seemed,—
    So holy are the vanished years.
    But then her cheeks were under tears:
It was on them the moonlight gleamed.

XXXI

Her sobbings at his bosom fall;
    Fonder than words can tell, they say
    Her heart was his, half love, half play,
But now all love she gives it all.

XXXII

'Twas she, your mother ! While she hung
  Her head, and hid her tears, and crept
  To me, as one who, erring, wept ;
Wept more the closer that she clung ;

XXXIII

She seemed an infant in my arms—
  Kissed me as would a child bereaved :
  And then, as 'twere for joy, she grieved—
Her heart released from its alarms.

XXXIV

God bless you, Rose ! That loving face—
  Could she but see it ! Well I knew
  Her thoughts when last she looked at you,
Who now have grown up in her place.

XXXV

Ah, leave me, Rose ! these memories stir
  Depths that you may not dream of, child !
  These tears till now your love has wiled ;
Leave me, that I may think of her.

THE SHEPHERDESS

I

By one whose heart kept watch was heard the fame
  Of a bright world that, like a ship of war,
Was launched in heaven beside the last that came
  O'er the sky's outer bar :
Her land Chaldea, she that blessed name
  Gave to the coming star.

II

Child of a lord, they called on her to reign
  O'er that old story-land whose shepherds deem
The stars a flock that studs a holy plain ;
  And she had learned in dream
That her loved land, through her, that star should
    gain
  And with its blessings teem.

III

But heartless deeds were of her father told
  Who the fair daughters, in the mountains born,
Had captured and to days of slavery sold
  Where bends the Golden Horn :
A shepherd chief, who robbed his neighbour's fold,
  And took the lamb unshorn.

IV

She bears her crook o'er living plains, her way
  Through tents in which the thoughtful shepherds
    dwell
Who watch the heavens where the bright grazers
  stray
  And think they hear the bell
Whose holy tinklings, as they softly play,
  The fates of men foretell.

V

So doth she haste to meet her shepherd-seers,
  And see the promised star that shall eclipse
The one which filled her father's land with tears,
  And learn from their own lips
The happy portents that to man it bears
  From the new heaven it skips.

VI

While Tigris and Euphrates still o'erleap
  Their shallow bounds her camel slowly goes,
When nigh her tent, on vengeful errand, creep
  Her father's olden foes,
And seize her, helpless, in her noon-day sleep
  While all her tribes repose.

VII

In a barred chamber, and in chains, a slave,
  She weeps with eyes upon the Golden Horn,
And thinks of far-off waters as they lave
  Blest homes in Capricorn,
Where happy beings find the Heaven that gave
  To her the star new-born.

VIII

Strangers have come and through her prison-gate
  They count her price and would her love allure ;
But her eyes restless watch and wide dilate ;
  Their look can none endure,
So wild in sorrow and so mild in hate,
  In majesty so pure.

IX

One comes towards whom the look of prayer she bends
  That seems to utter 'Thou, my star, arise !'
And while that heaven-adoring thought ascends
  New sorrows fill her eyes,
That tell how Love is dead and beauty ends
  When human pity dies !

X

All that he has, the mystic life he bears,
  What is their worth, her soul in slavery ?
He pays the ransom, breaks the chain she wears,
  As though some god were he :
Voiceless, she offers up to him the tears
  Her anguish has set free.

XI

Handmaids and armed protectors are at hand,
  All that to queenly power and pomp pertains,
And, passing waters from the stranger-land,
  Her star-roofed home she gains,
Where her sleek camels, crimson-girded, stand
  To bear her o'er the plains.

H

XII

In her slow path the faithful seers arrive
　　And with prophetic tidings bid her cheer:
That night, they tell, the older worlds shall strive,
　　As the new star comes near,
And into depths of unknown darkness dive
　　And find no other sphere.

XIII

But little heed gives she to their appeals:
　　The coming star, alas! not yet is found;
Deep-sighing in her silence, she feveals
　　A heart in slavery bound:
Her bonds are there, and there it is she feels
　　The chain about her wound.

XIV

'Mid joyous shouts she sees her open gates,
　　But enters not, up-gazing in the thought
That never sleeps or in her breast abates,
　　Where is the star she sought!
But now a greater seer her advent waits;
　　He hath the tidings brought.

XV

'The hour is come, the star is now in sight ;
　　Portents of blessed change the heavens bestrew :
The shepherds upward gaze, the air is bright,
　　The sky is gold and blue,
The ancient stars are on their downward flight
　　And others come anew.

XVI

' And in the shower of burning worlds, self-hurled
　　From heaven to heaven, a lord is on his way
Around whose hosts the golden dust is whirled,
　　While, in divine array,
Green floats his shepherd-banner, wide-unfurled,
　　With flocks thereon at play.'

XVII

The hour has come in clouds that hurry o'er
　　Her palace towers, and scatter while the rays
Of new-made light upon the valleys pour ;
　　While flocks awake and graze,
And shepherds sing and the new star adore :
　　But she, beholding, prays.

XVIII

The seer of seers stands forth, he takes her hands;
 He cries, 'Thy star is come!   Be it to thee
A rich reward and to these teeming lands;
 The lord, who made thee free,
Now in his earthly place before thee stands,
 Thy guiding-star to be.'

XIX

She looks at heaven; afar the cloud-vane drifts;
 Her face is pale, he comes, the lord is found:
She kneels, once more his slave; the stranger lifts
 The virgin from the ground,
And offers up for sacred wedding gifts
 The chains her heart had bound.

FAREWELL TO NATURE

Vain love for Nature!   How these heartaches rust
Into the soul as we return to dust!
Hope's shadow only masks our eventide,
Feigning to lead us to its brighter side,
While yet the mellowing skies that wondrous grow,
Seem left in waiting for the dead below.
But those tranced sunsets,—little they avail,
None travel hence in their alluring trail;
All is a dream, an ancient dream, the same
From the first mortal to the last that came.
Yet could we but for once our eyes unclose
When through the distant days the pageant goes!
Familiar vision, and so soon to be
Entombed within the dead eternity.

Doth Nature know our dream, or is the mind
A passing breath her beauty leaves behind?

Ah ! not for this our grateful souls have wrought
Around her sphere a universe of thought.
'Tis she inspires our dreams, but no reply
Vouchsafes the loving hearts that for her die,
Who only pray, when life's surprise is o'er,
They may partake a glimpse of her once more.
Is it too late ?   She sees not to the end ;
What she hath done she never can amend .
Yet once by us beloved, once only known,
She seems from all the past to be our own.

Last wish of age !   How sweet one glance would be
Even from the sod the olden haunts to see ;
To watch the long-drawn wavelets as they reach
The silent plains of the deserted beach ;
To look where light once was, if but to know
Of its faint struggle through the winnowed snow.
Ah ! whence this dream that like the cuckoo-guest
Pleads in such winning accents for a nest,
And with its cloud-note ever on us calls,
And though it passes the fond heart enthralls ?

Little it seems, this wish, when oft our sight
Tires of the world, yet what a fresh delight

Were it sometimes in death those scenes to view,
The olden scenes that to our youth were new,
To linger o'er a sound whose murmurs swell
Upon the heart,—the tinkling village bell,—
To find that all was safe, all gliding on
In beauty's leisure ways though we were gone;
To see brave Nature in her perilous scheme
Advance without our help, without our dream.
At least 'twould hold ajar death's open door
To think our love was honoured evermore,—
In dying, on the forward thought to dwell
That it was not our very last farewell.

Could hope unveil and not its mystic fire
Be lost among the embers of desire !
Ill though desponding hearts their burden bear,
Is not the soul the master of despair ?
Is this great life, hard won, achieved in vain,
Is good once found to never be again ?
Ask of the worlds if they their path forget,
Ask hope that never ends, its time to set.
One deep desire throughout all being cries,
And this is hope, our future in disguise.

O living lamp, O Hope, the only Seer;
Of Nature's after-time the pioneer,
Keep in advance across our starless way,
Be the new morrow of our orphan day!

THE POET'S FEAST

THE golden feast for jovial souls prepare
   Whose wants the wants of nature far exceed ;
   The nectar of the sun such palates need ;
To them the fatted calf is vulgar fare.
Earth's dripping fruits may wandering Arabs share
   Pleased with the pulp and juice whereon they
     feed ;
   And bread alone is still the poor man's meed,
Though milk abound and honey be to spare.
So dreams the Poet, with his crust content :
   The crumbs that from the rich man's table fall
To him are sorry signs of merriment
   To show the world has food enough for all.
At festive boards he has but little part—
To him 'twas given to feed on his own heart.

THE EXILE

I

THEY bore her to the northern snows
   Whose floods down ice-domed caverns run,
From lands where that calm river flows
   Whose depths decoy the vagrant sun,
Where palms o'er latticed shadows rise
With boughs that web the sultry skies.

II

Where roses climb the scent-steeped hills
   And channelled leaves with dew-drops flash,
Bending beneath the trickled rills
   That fall and the pink clusters splash;
Where aloe-flowers, all flaming red,
Like watch-fires o'er the summit spread.

III

They bore her to a desert plain
  Where the dry, creviced mosses cling,
Sand-sprinkled as by drizzling rain ;
  Where dark and ragged pine-boughs swing,
And the free cygnet in its flight
Darts with a meteor's wingèd light.

IV

Her father, last of mighty lords
  Whose deeds the war-like peasants tell,
Fearless had met the northern hordes
  And in the battle's frenzy fell.
Full-armed he sleeps, and still the brave
Salute him as they pass his grave.

V

Now young, she thinks not of her race
  But feels its glory and its pride.
She still recalls her mother's face
  Who in her stately sorrow died,
And those large eyes her image keep,
And dream beside it in love's sleep.

VI

Eyes that are of the sultry zone—
  That ofttimes in their musing moods
See rosy banks that seem their own
  Where lies the waste : her olive-woods,
Her sky with cypress-skirted folds,
All that she loves, her heart remoulds.

VII

As in a desert one red rose
  Seems like a garden full of bloom,
She charms the wilderness, and throws
  Her own bright colours o'er its gloom ;
Then at the falling cone's rebound
Pomegranates gild the enchanted ground.

VIII

And lest when dear illusions come
  They melt o'er-fast, she hides her eyes,
And feigns to see her native home,
  And shouts in play her soul's surprise.
So while the southern glory burns
The haunting vision still returns.

IX

When spring bursts o'er the wintry plain
   And violet skies dissolve in spray,
And marsh-pools echo drops of rain
   That o'er the bud's new secret play,
Her soul seems darting from her eyes
To snatch at nature's rhapsodies.

X

The serf who toils upon the road
   From waste to waste with back that bears
Across the steppes another's load,—
   With eyes that homeward gaze in tears,—
Chills not for long a heart that glows
In its own fire 'mid northern snows.

XI

Where plough may delve or harrow graze,
   She tramps beside the sluggish team
As fain to urge its tardy pace :
   And when she drifts into some dream
Her laugh, her look of childish glee,
Is still the joy of memory.

XII

But fears flash o'er her mellow eyes
   When gaunt sand-fountains, side by side,
Like giants in the distance rise,
   Pass slowly by and onward glide,
Like shadows from her father's land
That seek some rumoured icy strand.

XIII

Then day breaks through a sullen sky;
   The keen air shivers;—doth she know
The blackened clouds now sailing by
   Are freighted with the virgin snow?
Dark ships of winter that unload
The widespread famine they forbode.

XIV

The snow-flakes build a prison-wall
   That slants high o'er her window sill;
She watches while they slowly fall,
   Till heaven appears a sinking hill,
And darkness gathers o'er her mind:
Home is too far for hope to find.

XV

In new despair she sees heaven's sand
　　Has drifted o'er her cottage gate !
She fears that now her native land
　　Is like the desert desolate.
The snow still falls and still it clings,
Soft dropped like insects' broken wings.

XVI

Through the strange dusk she hears the shriek
　　Of trees snapped by the dreaded wind ;
The casements shake, the rafters creak ;
　　Ah ! could she now her mother find !
With timid wings too weak for flight
She hangs upon the edge of night.

XVII

A wind's moan utters, 'Stir and go':
　　Upon its gust she seems to glide
Towards lands beyond the falling snow
　　But reaches not its further side.
She drops on the cold hilly steeps
And in her distant reverie sleeps.

XVIII

No longer now the large-eyed child,
　　Who draws her charm so fresh from heaven,
Gives up its beauty to the wild ;
　　The spell of infant faith is riven :
Where the sun's tender rays were sown
Stones have sprung up and ice-fields grown.

XIX

The spring still comes, when shallow snows
　　Melt o'er a crisping flame of green
Wherein the nestled herbage glows
　　Through its white shell,—but there is seen
A heart that still unthawed remains ;
An exile of the loveless plains.

XX

When winter's sun through summer shines,
　　The joys are banished that she brought :
For home, not dreams of home, she pines ;
　　Thought is the food of famished thought.
It is her heart-corroding hour :
The rose-tree is without a flower.

XXI

She feeds in broken reveries
   On her chilled soul: within the light
Of those black lashes, those dark eyes,
   The paling cheek seems over-bright,
With lips, like hanging fruit, whose hue
Is ruby 'neath a bloom of blue.

XXII

The friends who love her as their own
   Stir self-upbraidings in her breast,
For in their midst she is alone
   And in their peace is without rest.
Is there some home by them forgot?
Exiles they seem and suffer not.

XXIII

Their native games to her impart
   A fitful joy, that sad appears,
Only because her eyes and heart
   Are vacant, and have room for tears.
She knows not yet 'tis love's first throe:
The snowdrop breaking through the snow.

I

XXIV

At length comes one whose love ere told
  Seems wafted o'er a flowery plain,
And brings her back that charm of old:
  The days of childhood live again;
Griefs softened into joys return;
In love's new-kindled incense burn.

XXV

In silver-crimson trappings gay,
  His tinkling barbs with billowy manes
Toss their strong necks before his sleigh—
  And he has crossed the snowy plains.
She hails him, and, with heart aflame,
She wonders how such passion came.

XXVI

Beauty and man's strong soul are his.
  Be the earth bare, paved o'er with ice,
'Tis full even to its dome in bliss:
  The desert is her paradise,
Where now the hourly deepening sky
Rains down on her love's mystery.

XXVII

She hears his love and hears no more.
  As waves might cease to beat, as winds
Might drop away on some charmed shore,
  The word a soul-deep echo finds—
All her fond life is without breath,
And sinks away in rapturous death.

XXVIII

New paths to home are overlaid
  With such deep sunshine, not a tree
In densest woods can cast a shade.
  Her glorious soul again is free,—
Free in those bonds of love that wind
In bliss about the heart they bind.

XXIX

Warmer than in its childhood's flush
  Her cheek in this new passion glows;
Not softer is the fitful blush
  Of lily 'neath the swaying rose.
Her head droops not as when she pined,
Now bowed in love's own southern wind.

XXX

A sun of passion is above ;
   Her home is here,—in cloudless eyes
She sees the birth-place of her love,
   And snows dissolve in burning skies.
Palm-leaves above her seem to bow
When bridal roses wreathe her brow.

THE SIBYL

A MAID who mindful of her playful time
  Steps to her summer, bearing childhood on
To woman's beauty, heedless of her prime :
  The early day but not the pastime gone :
She is the Sibyl, uttering a doom
Out of her spotless bloom.

She is the Sibyl; seek not, then, her voice ;—
  A laugh, a song, a sorrow, but thy share,
With woes at hand for many who rejoice
  That she shall utter; that shall many hear ;
That warn all hearts who seek of her their fates,
Her love but one awaits.

III

She is the Sibyl; days that distant lie
    Bend to the promise that her word shall give;
Already hath she eyes that prophesy,
    For of her beauty shall all beauty live:
Unknown to her, in her slow opening bloom,
She turns the leaves of doom.

THE PAINTER

I

'Summer has done her work,' the painter cries,
  And saunters down his garden by the shore.
'The fig is cracked and dry; upon it lies,
  In crystals, the sweet oozing of its core.
The peach melts in its dusk and yellow bloom,
  Grapes cluster to the earth in diadems
  Of dripping purple; from their slender stems,
'Mid paler leaves, the dark-green citrons loom.

II

'Summer has done her work; she, lingering, sees
  Her shady places glare : yet cooler grow
The breezes as they stir the sunny trees
  Whose shaking twigs their ruby berries sow.
Ripe is the fairy-grass, we breathe its seeds,
  But, hanging o'er the rocks that belt the shore,
  Safe from the sea, above its bustling roar,
Here ripen, still, the blossom-swinging weeds.

III

'Pale cressets on the summer waters shine,
  No ripple there but flings its jet of fire.
Rich amber wrack still bronzing in the brine
  Is tossed ashore in daylight to expire.
Here wallowing waves the rocky shoal enwreathe,
  And in loose spray, cascades of bubbles fall,
  And steeps of watery, coral-mantled wall
Drink of the billow, and the sunshine breathe.

IV

'Summer has done her work, but mine remains.
  How shall I shape these ever-murmuring waves,
How interweave these rumours and refrains,
  These wind-tossed echoes of the listening caves?
The restless rocky roar, the billow's splash,
  And the all-hushing shingle—hark! it blends,
  In open melody that never ends,
The drone, the cavern-whisper, and the clash.'

V

'And this wide ruin of a once new shore
  Scooped by new waves to waves of solid rock,
Dark-shelving, white-veined, as if marbled o'er
  By the fresh surf still trickling block to block!

O worn-out waves of night, long set aside—
　　The moulded storm in dead, contending rage,—
　　Like monster-breakers of a by-gone age !
And now the gentle waters o'er you ride.

VI

' Can my hand darken in swift rings of flight
　　The air-path cut by the black sea-bird's wings,
Then fill the dubious track with influent light,
　　While to my eyes the vanished vision clings ?
While at their sudden whirr the billows start,
　　Can my hand hush the cymbal-sounding sea,
　　That breaks with louder roar its reverie
As those fast pinions into silence dart ?

VII

' Press on, ye summer waves, still gently swell,—
　　The rainbow's parent-waters overrun !
Can my poor brush your snaky greenness tell,
　　Raising your sidelong bellies to the sun ?
What touch can pour you in yon pool of blue
　　Circled with surging froth of liquid snow,
　　Which now dissolves to emerald, now below
Glazes the sunken rocks with umber hue ?

VIII

'Summer has done her work; dare I begin—
   Painting a desert, though my pencil craves
To intertwine all tints with heaven akin?
   Nature has flung her palette to the waves!
Then bid my eyes on cloudy landscape dwell,—
   Not revel in thy blaze, O beauteous scene!
   Between thy art and mine is nature's screen,—
Transparent only to the soul,—farewell!

IX

'Oh! could I paint thee with these ravished eyes,—
   Catch in my hollow palm thy overflow,
Who broadcast fling'st away thy witcheries!
   Yet would I not desponding turn and go.
Be it a feeble hand to thee I raise,
   'Tis still the worship of the soul within:
   Summer has done her work,—let mine begin,
Though as the grass it wither in thy blaze.'

THE SUN-WORSHIPPER

I

As a wild comet through the night she hies,
  Her face bent towards the temple of the sun,
With golden hair that on the darkness lies
  Like break of dawn when daylight, scarce begun,
  Meanders into flame whose flashes run
Along the lower skies.

II

Soon as the sun lifts up the morning haze
  She rushes towards him ; sinks unto the ground
And, clasping the all-shining Presence, prays
  In his first beams : again her god is found ;
  The startled shadows that her heart surround
Are dizzy in his rays.

III

'Thee I adore, O Sun! this heart is thine!
  The youth who blindly claims its ecstasy
Seeks not thy temple, honours not thy shrine;
    He kneels not, utters not his vows to thee,
    Who all the worlds beyond this world canst see,
And mak'st all things divine.'

IV

The sunflowers turn to heaven as still she kneels;
    Shall then her heart its coming vow deplore?
Not uttered yet, all utterance it reveals,
    And she restrains her ecstasy no more:
    Her burning lips the hasty vow outpour
Which her heart-trouble seals.

V

'Never, O Sun! till sinking in the west
    Thou risest where thy wondrous setting spreads,
While all who love thee slumber in thy rest,
    Shall he, who proudly in thy presence treads,
    Enthrall me in the light his beauty sheds,
Or wed me to his breast!'

VI

Silence has tongues ; she hears a sister say,
   ' List to the voice of thy companion-mind !
Thy love is still the same as yesterday ;
   It has not passed, it only lags behind,
   And thou art lonely as the wistful wind
Thou meet'st upon the way.'

VII

Yet she repeats her vow, her heart in pain,
   To draw some love from heaven, as from the well
Whose radiant springs she once craved not in vain:
   But ebbing hope allures her by its spell
   To past despair, on other days to dwell,—
And suffer them again.

VIII

Across the hills of heliotrope she creeps,
   Or winds within the many-shadowed wolds,
Till once again the sun her pathway sweeps,
   And from her weary feet the way withholds ;
   The sacred flowers embrace her in their folds ;
From dawn to dawn she sleeps.

IX

She sleeps; so still, not even her shadow veers,
  Save when from side to side the moonflood roves;
But in sky-dreams the sun to her appears,
  Yet with the visage of the one she loves;—
  All through her sleep in phantom light he moves,
And still that face he bears.

X

She sleeps, and with the beaming of a bride
  Beholds that face; ah! never to be wed!
Yet why a tear, no sorrow shall betide:
  Though distant borne, his rays on her are shed;
  Her soul, along his way of glory sped,
Shall in his light abide.

XI

She wakes up with the sun, but in his rise
  Sees the rich twilight of her love-dream wane:
Day seems to sink in the deserted skies,
  Whose broken, many-coloured beams remain
  As of her dream whose night comes back again;
'Twas dawn had closed her eyes.

XII

The cloud-slopes blossom still, but cold and lone ;
  Down them she floated in those heavenly dreams,
And still the veil that o'er her slumbers shone
    Hangs gold-wrought in the fervour of those beams.
    She kneels while watching the last fading gleams
O'er the grey twilight thrown.

XIII

With speechless lips she questions the chill blaze :
  Behold the sun returns ; that brighter flush
Were surely day ?   Yet she mistrusts her gaze
    Though the light widens and with lordly rush
    The sun bursts forth in morning's youthful blush
And floods the heaven with rays.

XIV

Trembling she sees the paleness of her face
  In those white clouds which now the sun surround,
Who doth in heaven his spectral way retrace.
    Behold, the days brought back, the hours unwound,
    The angry sun unto the zenith bound
And the pale moon replace !

XV

Perplexed, all lost, she staggers to the height
   Where the twelve pillars in their beauty shine,
The temple circling in the blessed light;
   There prostrate doth she o'er her vow repine;
   But fears to meet the arbiter divine
Who banishes the night.

XVI

From the lone steps at length she looks above:
   Behold, the face is there that filled her dreams;
The youth adored, triumphant o'er her love,
   There radiant shines amid descending beams;
   His lustrous hair in the rich sunshine streams,
With golden lights inwove.

XVII

She lifts her arms, she falls upon the face
   She loved in heaven; her yearning heart, too
      blest,
Doth in deep sobs its erring way retrace.
   All passion weeps, while gathers in her breast
   A bliss that bears her spirit to its rest
In that divine embrace.

THE INSCRUTABLE

I

DREAD under-life whose dreams
  Along the midnight rush,
Poured out like cavern-streams
  That from the darkness gush,
A murderous thought has issued forth to flood
A maiden's sleep in blood.

II

He that hath swum the heaven
  Of woman's loving eyes—
To him a dream is given,
  As helplessly he lies,
A dream that never nigh his thought had passed,
Till in that slumber cast.

K

III

He loves her and she loves,
  But stern her father's heart
That every passion moves
  Their holy hope to thwart.
Can they, meek sleepers, on dream-demons call
To burst the iron thrall?

IV

That night in dreams that sway
  The soul to shedding blood,
One hears his own voice say
  In sleep's half-weary mood,
'Take down your father's sword and quickly slide
The blade into his side.

V

'Disguise the seeming guilt,
  And bend his fingers round,
And put them on the hilt,
  And leave him to his wound.'
In that strange dream until the break of day,
Asleep the lover lay.

VI

He wakes, aghast; he strives
　　To get the vision hence
That into morning lives,
　　And fastens on his sense.
'Tis but a dream, but should her hand fulfil
His will within her will!

VII

She comes up wild and pale,
　　She wrings her hands in pain,
She utters with a wail—
　　'Who hath my father slain!
My anguished heart sobbed all night in its sleep;
I felt it sob and weep.

VIII

'I saw you while I slept,
　　And to my dream you spoke;
All night your words I kept,
　　I heard them when I woke:
"Take down your father's sword and quickly slide
The blade into his side.

IX

' " Disguise the seeming guilt,
  And bend his fingers round,
And put them on the hilt,
  And leave him to his wound."
O the false voice, that it so true should seem
In that unthought-of dream !

X

' I hurried to the bed,
  I saw that he was slain,
I saw the blood was shed,
  I saw the deep,—deep stain.
His sword was in his side,—thrust,—to the hilt,—
His fingers took the guilt.'

THE WEDDING RING

LADY

'Give me a ring, good jeweller,
 By no one worn before,
And you shall boast you gave it her
 Who wears it evermore.'

JEWELLER

'Then it shall be a ruby ring,
 With hoop of richest gold,
And it shall be my offering
 For benefits of old.'

LADY

'A ruby ring it must not be,
 Which is a thing to shine;
An iron ring is best for me,
 No other can be mine.'

JEWELLER

' But surely such a ring 'twere sad
   To see a lady wear
Among her guests in jewels clad,
   And she so young and fair.'

LADY

' An iron ring is all I crave
   Upon my wedding night,
For I must wear it in the grave,
   Where it is out of sight.'

JEWELLER

' Is it to be a ring to bind
   Your heart in wedlock's bond,
Or but to link the day behind
   And days that are beyond ? '

LADY

' It is to link me to his peace
   Who is not far away ;
And when her lonely term may cease,
   The bride shall with him stay.'

JEWELLER

'Who is this bridegroom you would wed,
　And yet for ever mourn,
As though you would espouse the dead,
　Who never can return ? '

LADY

' It is the dead I would espouse,
　With him lie side by side ;
There is a chamber in his house
　He furnished for his bride.'

LET THE DEAD BURY THEIR DEAD

Luke ix. 60

WHERE marshes venom-steeped the life-breeze taint
  And fitful meteors lap the watery wild,
A moon sinks in the cloud-mire, dazed and faint,
  Its pearly flush defiled,
Halo'd in sallow vapours like a saint
  Through paths impure beguiled.

But worse the gloom within the castle walls
  Where moans the lord whom pestilence devours :
The serfs awe-stricken flee his festering halls,
  The plague-star o'er him lowers,
On his glazed eyes the fatal glimmer falls
  While night weighs down his towers.

A crescent moon whose advent stays the pest
  Embalms the dead with heavenly obsequies,
But there are none to bear him to his rest,
  His body shroudless lies ;
Anointed not, by pious rites unblest,
  Unto the grave he cries.

A great half-moon now dominates the dome,
  With stern upbraidings yet not less benign :
But the blank gazers to his final home
  The dead dare not consign,
Lured on by sullen spectres of the gloam
  Who their own dead enshrine.

Again the drowsy marshes pillow night
  And darkness severs sky and earth in two,
But with a rush of cloud dispersing might
  A full moon hurries through ;
The corpse is shrouded as in living light,
  The castle walls look new.

The heaven is one blue wave ; it seems to break
  While lucid spray with dreamlight floods the air :
The coffins in the quickened graveyards quake,
  The bones know they are there,
And ghostly shades their buried depths forsake
  To gather in the glare.

As dusk descends, by its scared rays illumed,
  A soul-procession dense and denser grows :
Hearse after hearse night-horsed and sable-plumed
  A mirage heavenward throws :
The newly dead is by the dead entombed
  And nature has repose.

THE GOLDEN WEDDING

THE day but not the bride is come,
 As in her blossom-time;
But golden lights sustain the home
 She cherished in her prime.

May we not call upon the band?
 May we not ask the priest?
Our golden wedding is at hand,
 And we shall hold a feast.

But where is he in snow-white stole
 Who the old service read,
That made us one in heart and soul?
 Long, long has he been dead.

The bridesmaids clad in silken fold
 Who waited on the bride,
Where are they now? Their tale is told:
 Long, long ago they died.

Where is the groomsman, chosen friend,
  The true, the well-beloved;
His term, alas! is at an end;
  Too soon was he removed.

Where is the bride, ah! such a bride
  As every joy foretells?
I see her walking by my side,
  I hear the wedding-bells.

Where is she now? That we should say
  She did not live to know
How passed her silver wedding-day,
  So many years ago!

But come, and for your mother's sake,
  Though vain it were to weep,
Let us the silent feast partake,
  Her golden wedding keep.

Printed by T. and A. CONSTABLE, Printers to Her Majesty,
at the Edinburgh University Press.

List of Books

in

Belles Lettres

Elkin Mathews
& John Lane:
Publishers
and Vendors of
Choice & Rare
Editions in
Belles Lettres.

ALL BOOKS IN THIS CATALOGUE
ARE PUBLISHED AT NET PRICES

1894

Telegraphic Address—
'BODLEIAN, LONDON'

A WORD must be said for the manner in which the publishers have produced the volume (*i.e.* "The Earth Fiend"), a sumptuous folio, printed by CONSTABLE, the etchings on Japanese paper by MR. GOULDING. The volume should add not only to MR. STRANG'S fame but to that of MESSRS. ELKIN MATHEWS AND JOHN LANE, who are rapidly gaining distinction for their beautiful editions of belles-lettres.'—*Daily Chronicle*, Sept. 24, 1892.

Referring to MR. LE GALLIENNE'S 'English Poems' *and* 'Silhouettes' by MR. ARTHUR SYMONS :—'We only refer to them now to note a fact which they illustrate, and which we have been observing of late, namely, the recovery to a certain extent of good taste in the matter of printing and binding books. These two books, which are turned out by MESSRS. ELKIN MATHEWS AND JOHN LANE, are models of artistic publishing, and yet they are simplicity itself. The books with their excellent printing and their very simplicity make a harmony which is satisfying to the artistic sense.'—*Sunday Sun*, Oct. 2, 1892.

'MR. LE GALLIENNE is a fortunate young gentleman. I don't know by what legerdemain he and his publishers work, but here, in an age as stony to poetry as the ages of Chatterton and Richard Savage, we find the full edition of his book sold before publication. How is it done, MESSRS. ELKIN MATHEWS AND JOHN LANE? for, without depreciating MR. LE GALLIENNE'S sweetness and charm, I doubt that the marvel would have been wrought under another publisher. These publishers, indeed, produce books so delightfully that it must give an added pleasure to the hoarding of first editions.'—KATHARINE TYNAN in *The Irish Daily Independent*.'

'To MESSRS. ELKIN MATHEWS AND JOHN LANE almost more than to any other, we take it, are the thanks of the grateful singer especially due; for it is they who have managed, by means of limited editions and charming workmanship, to impress book-buyers with the belief that a volume may have an æsthetic and commercial value. They have made it possible to speculate in the latest discovered poet, as in a new company—with the difference that an operation in the former can be done with three half-crowns.'

St. James's Gazette.

List of Books

IN

BELLES LETTRES

(*Including some Transfers*)

PUBLISHED BY

Elkin Mathews and John Lane

𝕿𝖍𝖊 𝕭𝖔𝖉𝖑𝖊𝖞 𝕳𝖊𝖆𝖉

VIGO STREET, LONDON, W.

N.B.—The Authors and Publishers reserve the right of reprinting any book in this list if a second edition is called for, except in cases where a stipulation has been made to the contrary, and of printing a separate edition of any of the books for America irrespective of the numbers to which the English editions are limited. The numbers mentioned do not include the copies sent for review or to the public libraries.

———————◆———————

ADAMS (FRANCIS).
ESSAYS IN MODERNITY. Cr. 8vo. 5s. net. [*In preparation.*

ALLEN (GRANT).
THE LOWER SLOPES: A Volume of Verse. 600 copies. Cr. 8vo. 5s. net. [*Immediately.*

ANTÆUS.
THE BACKSLIDER AND OTHER POEMS. 100 only. Small 4to. 7s. 6d. net. [*Very few remain.*

BEECHING (H. C.), J. W. MACKAIL, & J. B. B. NICHOLS.
LOVE IN IDLENESS. With Vignette by W. B. SCOTT. Fcap. 8vo, half vellum. 12s. net. [*Very few remain.*
Transferred by the Authors to the present Publishers.

BENSON (ARTHUR CHRISTOPHER).
POEMS.   550 copies.   Fcap. 8vo.   5s. net.
[Very few remain.

BENSON (EUGENE).
FROM THE ASOLAN HILLS : A Poem.   300 copies.   Imp.
16mo.   5s. net.   *[Very few remain.*

BINYON (LAURENCE).
POEMS.   16mo.   5s. net.   *[In preparation.*

BOURDILLON (F. W.).
A LOST GOD : A Poem.   With Illustrations by H. J. FORD.
500 copies.   8vo.   6s. net.   *[Very few remain.*

BOURDILLON (F. W.).
AILES D'ALOUETTE.   Poems printed at the private press
of Rev. H. DANIEL, Oxford.   100 only.   16mo.
£1, 10s. net.   *[Not published.*

BRIDGES (ROBERT).
THE GROWTH OF LOVE.   Printed in Fell's old English
type at the private press of Rev. H. DANIEL, Oxford.
100 only.   Fcap. 4to.   £2, 12s. 6d. net.
[Not published.

COLERIDGE (HON. STEPHEN).
THE SANCTITY OF CONFESSION : A Romance.   Second
Edition.   Crown 8vo.   3s. net.   *[A few remain.*

CRANE (WALTER).
RENASCENCE : A Book of Verse.   Frontispiece and 38
designs by the Author.
[Small paper edition out of print.
There remain a few large paper copies, fcap. 4to. £1, 1s. net.
And a few fcap. 4to, Japanese vellum.   £1, 15s. net.

CROSSING (WM.).
THE ANCIENT CROSSES OF DARTMOOR.   With 11 plates.
8vo, cloth.   4s. 6d. net.   *[Very few remain.*

DAVIDSON (JOHN).

PLAYS: An Unhistorical Pastoral ; A Romantic Farce ;
Bruce, a Chronicle Play ; Smith, a Tragic Farce ;
Scaramouch in Naxos, a Pantomime, with a Frontis-
piece, Title-page, and Cover Design by AUBREY
BEARDSLEY. 500 copies. Small 4to. 7s. 6d. net.
[*Immediately.*

DAVIDSON (JOHN).

FLEET STREET ECLOGUES. Second Edition. Fcap. 8vo,
buckram. 5s. net.

DAVIDSON (JOHN).

A RANDOM ITINERARY: Prose Sketches, with a Ballad.
Frontispiece, Title-page, and Cover Design by LAUR-
ENCE HOUSMAN. Fcap. 8vo. Uniform with 'Fleet
Street Eclogues.' 5s. net.

DAVIDSON (JOHN).

THE NORTH WALL. Fcap. 8vo. 2s. 6d. net.
*The few remaining copies transferred by the Author
to the present Publishers.*

DE GRUCHY (AUGUSTA).

UNDER THE HAWTHORN, AND OTHER VERSES. Frontispiece by WALTER CRANE. 300 copies. Crown 8vo.
5s. net.   [*Very few remain.*
Also 30 copies on Japanese vellum. 15s. net.

DE TABLEY (LORD).

POEMS, DRAMATIC AND LYRICAL. By JOHN LEICESTER
WARREN (Lord De Tabley). Illustrations and Cover
Design by C. S. RICKETTS. Second Edition.
Crown 8vo. 7s. 6d. net.

DIAL (THE).

No. 1 of the Second Series. Illustrations by RICKETTS,
SHANNON, PISSARRO. 200 only. 4to. £1, 1s. net.
[*Very few remain.*
The present series will be continued at irregular intervals.

EGERTON (GEORGE).

KEYNOTES : Short Stories. With Title-page by AUBREY
BEARDSLEY. Second Edition. Crown 8vo. 3s. 6d.
net.

FIELD (MICHAEL).

SIGHT AND SONG. (Poems on Pictures.) 400 copies.
Fcap. 8vo. 5s. net.   [*Very few remain.*

FIELD (MICHAEL).

STEPHANIA : A Trialogue in Three Acts. 250 copies.
Pott 4to. 6s. net.   [*Very few remain.*

GALE (NORMAN).

ORCHARD SONGS. Fcap. 8vo. With Title-page and
Cover Design by J. ILLINGWORTH KAY. 5s. net.

Also a Special Edition limited in number on hand-made paper
bound in English vellum. £1, 1s. net

GARNETT (RICHARD).

A VOLUME OF POEMS. 350 copies. Crown 8vo. With
Title-page designed by J. ILLINGWORTH KAY. 5s. net.

GOSSE (EDMUND).

THE LETTERS OF THOMAS LOVELL BEDDOES. Now
first edited. Pott 8vo. 5s. net.

[*Immediately.*

GRAHAME (KENNETH).

PAGAN PAPERS : A Volume of Essays. Fcap. 8vo.
5s. net.

GREENE (G. A.).

ITALIAN LYRISTS OF TO-DAY. Translations in the
original metres from about thirty-five living Italian
poets, with bibliographical and biographical notes.
Crown 8vo. 5s. net.

HAKE (DR. T. GORDON).

A SELECTION FROM HIS POEMS. Edited by Mrs.
MEYNELL. With a Portrait after D. G. ROSSETTI.
Crown 8vo. 5s. net. *[Immediately.*

HALLAM (ARTHUR HENRY).

THE POEMS, together with his essay 'On Some of the
Characteristics of Modern Poetry and on the Lyrical
Poems of ALFRED TENNYSON.' Edited, with an
Introduction, by RICHARD LE GALLIENNE. 550
copies. Fcap. 8vo. 5s. net. *[Very few remain.*

HAMILTON (COL. IAN).

THE BALLAD OF HADJI AND OTHER POEMS. Etched
Frontispiece by WM. STRANG. 50 copies. Fcap. 8vo.
3s. net.
Transferred by the Author to the present Publishers.

HAYES (ALFRED).

THE VALE OF ARDEN AND OTHER POEMS. With Title-
page and Cover Design by LAURENCE HOUSMAN.
Fcap. 8vo. 5s. net. *[In preparation.*

HICKEY (EMILY H.).

VERSE TALES, LYRICS AND TRANSLATIONS. 300 copies.
Imp. 16mo. 5s. net.

HORNE (HERBERT P.).

DIVERSI COLORES : Poems. With ornaments by the
Author. 250 copies. 16mo. 5s. net.

IMAGE (SELWYN).

CAROLS AND POEMS. With decorations by H. P. HORNE.
250 copies. 16mo. 5s. net. *[In preparation.*

JAMES (W. P.).

ROMANTIC PROFESSIONS : A Volume of Essays, with Title-
page by J. ILLINGWORTH KAY. Crown 8vo. 5s. net.
[Immediately.

JOHNSON (EFFIE).

IN THE FIRE AND OTHER FANCIES. Frontispiece by WALTER CRANE. 500 copies. Imp. 16mo. 3s. 6d. net.

JOHNSON (LIONEL).

THE ART OF THOMAS HARDY: Six Essays. With Etched Portrait by WM. STRANG, and Bibliography by JOHN LANE. Crown 8vo. 5s. 6d. net.

Also 150 copies, large paper, with proofs of the portrait. £1, 1s. net. [*Very shortly.*

JOHNSON (LIONEL).

A VOLUME OF POEMS. Fcap. 8vo. 5s. net. [*In preparation.*

KEATS (JOHN).

THREE ESSAYS, now issued in book form for the first time. Edited by H. BUXTON FORMAN. With Life-mask by HAYDON. Fcap. 4to. 10s. 6d. net. [*Very few remain.*

LEATHER (R. K.).

VERSES. 250 copies. Fcap. 8vo. 3s. net. *Transferred by the Author to the present Publishers.*

LEATHER (R. K.), & RICHARD LE GALLIENNE.

THE STUDENT AND THE BODY-SNATCHER AND OTHER TRIFLES. [*Small paper edition out of print.* There remain a very few of the 50 large paper copies. 7s. 6d. net.

LE GALLIENNE (RICHARD).

PROSE FANCIES. With a Portrait of the Author. Cr. 8vo. 5s. net.

Also a limited large paper edition. 12s. 6d. net. [*In preparation.*

LE GALLIENNE (RICHARD).

THE BOOK BILLS OF NARCISSUS. An Account rendered by RICHARD LE GALLIENNE. Second Edition. Crown 8vo, buckram. 3s. 6d. net.

LE GALLIENNE (RICHARD).

ENGLISH POEMS. Third Edition, cr. 8vo. 5s. net.

LE GALLIENNE (RICHARD).

GEORGE MEREDITH : Some Characteristics. With a Bibliography (much enlarged) by JOHN LANE, portrait, etc. Third Edition. Crown 8vo. 5s. 6d. net.

LE GALLIENNE (RICHARD).

THE RELIGION OF A LITERARY MAN. Cr. 8vo. 3rd thousand. 3s. 6d. net.

Also a special rubricated edition on hand-made paper. 8vo. 10s. 6d. net.

LETTERS TO LIVING ARTISTS.

500 copies. Fcap. 8vo. 3s. 6d. net.   [*Very few remain.*

MARSTON (PHILIP BOURKE).

A LAST HARVEST : LYRICS AND SONNETS FROM THE BOOK OF LOVE. Edited by LOUISE CHANDLER MOULTON. 500 copies. Fcap. 8vo. 5s. net.

Also 50 copies on large paper, hand-made. 10s. 6d. net.
[*Very few remain.*

MARTIN (W. WILSEY).

QUATRAINS, LIFE'S MYSTERY AND OTHER POEMS. 16mo. 2s. 6d. net.   [*Very few remain.*

MARZIALS (THEO.).

THE GALLERY OF PIGEONS AND OTHER POEMS. Fcap. 8vo. 4s. 6d. net.   [*Very few remain.*
Transferred by the Author to the present Publishers.

MEYNELL (MRS.), (ALICE C. THOMPSON).

POEMS. Second Edition. Fcap. 8vo. 3s. 6d. net. A few of the 50 large paper copies (First Edition) remain, 12s. 6d. net.

MEYNELL (MRS.).
>THE RHYTHM OF LIFE, AND OTHER ESSAYS. Second Edition. Fcap. 8vo. 3s. 6d. net. A few of the 50 large paper copies (First Edition) remain. 12s. 6d. net.

MURRAY (ALMA).
>PORTRAIT AS BEATRICE CENCI. With critical notice containing four letters from ROBERT BROWNING. 8vo, wrapper. 2s. net.

NETTLESHIP (J. T.).
>ROBERT BROWNING: Essays and Thoughts. Third Edition. Crown 8vo. 5s. 6d. net. Half a dozen of the Whatman large paper copies (First Edition) remain. £1, 1s. net.

NOBLE (JAS. ASHCROFT).
>THE SONNET IN ENGLAND AND OTHER ESSAYS. Title-page and Cover Design by AUSTIN YOUNG. 600 copies. Crown 8vo. 5s. net.
>Also 50 copies large paper. 12s. 6d. net.

NOEL (HON. RODEN).
>POOR PEOPLE'S CHRISTMAS. 250 copies. 16mo. 1s. net.
>*[Very few remain.*

OXFORD CHARACTERS.
>A series of lithographed portraits by WILL ROTHENSTEIN, with text by F. YORK POWELL and others. To be issued monthly in term. Each number will contain two portraits. Part I. contains portraits of SIR HENRY ACLAND and Mr. W. A. L. FLETCHER, and Part II. of Mr. ROBINSON K. ELLIS, and LORD ST. CYRES. 200 copies only, folio, wrapper, 5s. net per part; 25 special copies containing proof impressions of the portraits signed by the artist, 10s. 6d. net per part.

PINKERTON (PERCY).
>GALEAZZO: A Venetian Episode and other Poems. Etched Frontispiece. 16mo. 5s. net.
>*[Very few remain.*
>*Transferred by the Author to the present Publishers.*

RADFORD (DOLLIE).

SONGS. A New Volume of Verse.   [*In preparation.*

RADFORD (ERNEST).

CHAMBERS TWAIN. Frontispiece by WALTER CRANE.
250 copies. Imp. 16mo. 5s. net.
Also 50 copies large paper. 10s. 6d. net.   [*Very few remain.*

RHYMERS' CLUB, THE BOOK OF THE.

A second series is in preparation.

SCHAFF (DR. P.).

LITERATURE AND POETRY: Papers on Dante, etc.
Portrait and Plates, 100 copies only. 8vo. 10s. net.

SCOTT (WM. BELL).

A POET'S HARVEST HOME: WITH AN AFTERMATH.
300 copies. Fcap. 8vo. 5s. net. [*Very few remain.*
*** *Will not be reprinted.*

SHAW (A. D. L.).

THE HAPPY WANDERER. Poems. Fcap. 8vo. 5s. net.
[*In preparation.*

STODDARD (R. H.).

THE LION'S CUB; WITH OTHER VERSE. Portrait.
100 copies only, bound in an illuminated Persian
design. Fcap. 8vo. 5s. net.   [*Very few remain.*

SYMONDS (JOHN ADDINGTON).

IN THE KEY OF BLUE, AND OTHER PROSE ESSAYS.
Cover designed by C. S. RICKETTS. Second Edition.
Thick Crown 8vo. 8s. 6d. net.

THOMPSON (FRANCIS).

A VOLUME OF POEMS. With Frontispiece, Title-page
and Cover Design by LAURENCE HOUSMAN. Second
Edition. Pott 4to. 5s. net.

TODHUNTER (JOHN).

A SICILIAN IDYLL. Frontispiece by WALTER CRANE.
250 copies. Imp. 16mo. 5s. net.
Also 50 copies large paper, fcap. 4to. 10s. 6d. net.
[*Very few remain.*

TOMSON (GRAHAM R.).

AFTER SUNSET. A Volume of Poems. With Title-page and
Cover Design by R. ANNING BELL. Fcap. 8vo.   5s.
net.

Also a limited large paper edition.   12s. 6d. net.   [*In preparation.*

TREE (H. BEERBOHM).

THE IMAGINATIVE FACULTY : A Lecture delivered at the
Royal Institution.   With portrait of Mr. TREE from
an unpublished drawing by the Marchioness of Granby.
Fcap. 8vo, boards.   2s. 6d. net.

TYNAN HINKSON (KATHARINE).

CUCKOO SONGS.   With Title-page and Cover Design by
LAURENCE HOUSMAN.   500 copies.   Fcap. 8vo.   5s.
net.   [*In preparation.*

VAN DYKE (HENRY).

THE POETRY OF TENNYSON.   Third Edition, enlarged.
Crown 8vo.   5s. 6d. net.

*The late Laureate himself gave valuable aid in correcting
various details.*

WATSON (WILLIAM).

THE ELOPING ANGELS : A Caprice.   Second Edition.
Square 16mo, buckram.   3s. 6d. net.

WATSON (WILLIAM).

EXCURSIONS IN CRITICISM : being some Prose Recrea-
tions of a Rhymer.   Second Edition.   Cr. 8vo.   5s. net.

WATSON (WILLIAM).

THE PRINCE'S QUEST, AND OTHER POEMS.   With a
Bibliographical Note added.   Second Edition.   Fcap.
8vo.   4s. 6d. net.

WEDMORE (FREDERICK).

PASTORALS OF FRANCE—RENUNCIATIONS.   A volume of
Stories.   Title-page by JOHN FULLEYLOVE, R.I.
Crown 8vo.   5s. net.

*A few of the large paper copies of Renunciations (First Edition)
remain.   10s. 6d. net.*

WICKSTEED (P. H.).
DANTE. Six Sermons. Third Edition. Crown 8vo. 2s. net.

WILDE (OSCAR).
THE SPHINX. A poem decorated throughout in line and colour, and bound in a design by CHARLES RICKETTS. 250 copies. £2, 2s. net. 25 copies large paper. £5, 5s. net. [*Very shortly.*

WILDE (OSCAR).
The incomparable and ingenious history of Mr. W. H., being the true secret of Shakespear's sonnets now for the first time here fully set forth, with initial letters and cover design by CHARLES RICKETTS. 500 copies. 10s. 6d. net.
Also 50 copies large paper. 21s. net.   [*In preparation.*

WILDE (OSCAR).
DRAMATIC WORKS, now printed for the first time with a specially designed Title-page and binding to each volume, by CHARLES SHANNON. 500 copies. Small 4to. 7s. 6d. net per vol.
Also 50 copies large paper. 15s. net per vol.
Vol. I. LADY WINDERMERE'S FAN : A Comedy in Four Acts. [*Ready.*
Vol. II. A WOMAN OF NO IMPORTANCE : A Comedy in Four Acts. [*Shortly.*
Vol. III. THE DUCHESS OF PADUA : A Blank Verse Tragedy in Five Acts. [*In preparation.*

WILDE (OSCAR).
SALOMÉ : A Tragedy in one Act, done into English. With 11 Illustrations, title-page, and Cover Design by AUBREY BEARDSLEY. 500 copies. Small 4to. 15s. net.
Also 100 copies, large paper. 30s. net.   [*Shortly.*

WYNNE (FRANCES).
WHISPER. A Volume of Verse. With a Memoir by Katharine Tynan and a Portrait added. Fcap. 8vo. 2s. 6d. net.
Transferred by the Author to the present Publishers.

The Hobby Horse

A new series of this illustrated magazine will be published quarterly by subscription, under the Editorship of Herbert P. Horne. Subscription £1 per annum, post free, for the four numbers. Quarto, printed on hand-made paper, and issued in a limited edition to subscribers only. The Magazine will contain articles upon Literature, Music, Painting, Sculpture, Architecture, and the Decorative Arts; Poems; Essays; Fiction; original Designs; with reproductions of pictures and drawings by the old masters and contemporary artists. There will be a new title-page and ornaments designed by the Editor. Among the contributors to the Hobby Horse are:

The late MATTHEW ARNOLD.
LAURENCE BINYON.
WILFRID BLUNT.
FORD MADOX BROWN.
The late ARTHUR BURGESS.
E. BURNE-JONES, A.R.A.
AUSTIN DOBSON.
RICHARD GARNETT, LL.D.
A. J. HIPKINS, F.S.A.
SELWYN IMAGE.
LIONEL JOHNSON.
RICHARD LE GALLIENNE.
SIR F. LEIGHTON, Bart., P.R.A.
T. HOPE McLACHLAN.
MAY MORRIS.
C. HUBERT H. PARRY, Mus. Doc.
A. W. POLLARD.

F. YORK POWELL.
CHRISTINA G. ROSSETTI.
W. M. ROSSETTI.
JOHN RUSKIN, D.C.L., LL.D.
FREDERICK SANDYS.
The late W. BELL SCOTT.
FREDERICK J. SHIELDS.
J. H. SHORTHOUSE.
The late JAMES SMETHAM.
SIMEON SOLOMON.
A. SOMERVELL.
The late J. ADDINGTON SYMONDS.
KATHARINE TYNAN.
G. F. WATTS, R.A.
FREDERICK WEDMORE.
OSCAR WILDE.

Prospectuses on Application.

THE BODLEY HEAD, VIGO STREET, LONDON, W.

'Nearly every book put out by Messrs. Elkin Mathews & John Lane, at the Sign of the Bodley Head, is a satisfaction to the special senses of the modern bookman for bindings, shapes, types, and papers.   They have surpassed themselves, and registered a real achievement in English bookmaking by the volume of " Poems, Dramatic and Lyrical," of Lord De Tabley.'
Newcastle Daily Chronicle.

' A ray of hopefulness is stealing again into English poetry after the twilight greys of Clough and Arnold and Tennyson. Even unbelief wears braver colours.   Despite the jeremiads, which are the dirges of the elder gods, England is still a nest of singing-birds (*teste* the Catalogue of Elkin Mathews and John Lane).' —Mr. ZANGWILL in *Pall Mall Magazine.*

'All Messrs. Mathews & Lane's Books are so beautifully printed and so tastefully issued, that it rejoices the heart of a book-lover to handle them ; but they have shown their sound judgment not less markedly in the literary quality of their publications.   The choiceness of form is not inappropriate to the matter, which is always of something more than ephemeral worth.   This was a distinction on which the better publishers at one time prided themselves ; they never lent their names to trash ; but some names associated with worthy traditions have proved more than once a delusion and a snare.   The record of Messrs. Elkin Mathews & John Lane is perfect in this respect, and their imprint is a guarantee of the worth of what they publish.'—*Birmingham Daily Post*, Nov. 6, 1893.

' One can nearly always be certain when one sees on the title-page of any given book the name of Messrs Elkin Mathews & John Lane as being the publishers thereof that there will be something worth reading to be found between the boards.'— *World.*